D0351280

SPECIAL MESSAGE TO READERS

THE ULVERSCROFT FOUNDATION
(registered UK charity number 264873)

was established in 1972 to provide funds for
research, diagnosis and treatment of eye diseases.
Examples of major projects funded by
the Ulverscroft Foundation are:-

- The Children's Eye Unit at Moorfields Eye Hospital, London
- The Ulverscroft Children's Eye Unit at Great Ormond Street Hospital for Sick Children
- Funding research into eye diseases and treatment at the Department of Ophthalmology, University of Leicester
- The Ulverscroft Vision Research Group, Institute of Child Health
- Twin operating theatres at the Western Ophthalmic Hospital, London
- The Chair of Ophthalmology at the Royal Australian College of Ophthalmologists

You can help further the work of the Foundation
by making a donation or leaving a legacy.
Every contribution is gratefully received. If you
would like to help support the Foundation or
require further information, please contact:

THE ULVERSCROFT FOUNDATION
The Green, Bradgate Road, Anstey
Leicester LE7 7FU, England
Tel: (0116) 236 4325

website: www.foundation.ulverscroft.com

SHOTGUN CHARADE

Cowboy Laramie Juke helps out a new buddy whose family is being harassed by Highspade Jack Daley, the unscrupulous Mayor of Jacinto. Attempting to get rid of the Cavendish clan, who have discovered a rich gold seam — the source of which hides beneath his own land — Daley has hired the notorious Shotgun Murphy. But when Juke arrives in Jacinto, he is mistaken for the gunman . . . leading to a deadly encounter where nothing is as it seems, and no one can be trusted.

ETHAN FLAGG

SHOTGUN CHARADE

Complete and Unabridged

LINFORD
Leicester

First published in Great Britain in 2013 by
Robert Hale Limited
London

First Linford Edition
published 2015
by arrangement with
Robert Hale Limited
London

A catalogue record for this book is available
from the British Library.

ISBN 978–1–4448–2644–9

Published by
F. A. Thorpe (Publishing)
Anstey, Leicestershire

Set by Words & Graphics Ltd.
Anstey, Leicestershire
Printed and bound in Great Britain by
T. J. International Ltd., Padstow, Cornwall

This book is printed on acid-free paper

1

Cleaned Out

Jubilant cowpuncher Laramie Juke brought his mustang to a skittering halt outside the first saloon he encountered.

It was none other than Dodge City's renowned Long Branch. Laramie was one of ten drovers who had just been paid off. It had been a hard three months pushing 2,000 recalcitrant longhorns up the Chisholm Trail from Texas.

The Lazy K outfit were camped outside the town. Close by stood mounds of buffalo hides waiting to be processed. The rank odour of festering skins and sweaty cattle was impossible to ignore. But together, they had brought affluence to the settlement and were accordingly tolerated by the permanent residents.

By 1876 Dodge City was a bustling cow town with large herds arriving

almost daily during the summer season. It was the arrival of the Atchison and Topeka railroad in '72 that had ensured the town's prosperity.

But Dodge quickly became famous for all the wrong reasons, namely a perverse reputation for rowdy behaviour that frequently ended in violence.

Excessive consumption of hard liquor was the culprit. After months of gruelling labour devoid of earthly pleasures, the drovers were impatient for a good time. And nothing and nobody was going to stop them.

Shooting up the town became a favourite pastime.

It soon became apparent that the only way to curb the wild gunplay was to instigate a town ordinance which forbade the wearing of sidearms within the city limits. Tough marshals such as Wyatt Earp and Bat Masterson were employed to make sure that law and order was maintained.

As a result, the town council had been most effective in separating these

transitory yet raucous elements from the resident population. All new buildings offering such attractions had to be erected south of the railroad. Thereafter, a saying emerged claiming that lawless folk had been brought up on the wrong side of the tracks.

So it was that as soon as Laramie Juke entered the Long Branch on that August day, he was accosted by a thickset deputy with the colourful handle of Rockpile Buzz Bickerstaff. And it certainly fitted the heavyset lawdog. He made no secret of the fact that his previous job had been as a guard supervising prison chain gangs.

'Hang your hogleg over yonder,' came the gravelly order as the big guy pointed to a line of gunbelts. 'Collect it when you leave town and not before.'

The unpopular ruling had certainly helped to curb the wayward use of firearms along Front Street. In the beginning, though, it hadn't prevented numerous shifty dudes from seeking to evade the order by concealing weapons

3

beneath their shirts. When caught they were unceremoniously tarred and feathered, then run out of town on a rail. A more humiliating punishment could not be imagined.

After that, only the very drunk or the foolhardy challenged the town's law enforcers.

'Sure thing,' concurred the easy-going cowpoke, unbuckling his rig.

Laramie was happy to comply. This was his first visit to Dodge. Making the acquaintance of the celebrated drinking den was a long sought-after ambition. Ira Kemp, who owned the Lazy K ranch, was a tartar when it came to the demon drink. A dyed-in-the-wool Baptist lay preacher, he had banned its use throughout the drive.

Two foolish saddle tramps who had hired on late were given a taste of Kemp's bull whip when they strayed from the temperance path.

The rancher had only discovered the route earlier in the spring. By heading for Dodge City he could chop two

weeks from the trail time. To a shrewd operator like Kemp, that was a big saving in money.

It had also meant that the hands were able to secure an extra bonus, which nobody was complaining about. The other Lazy K riders had headed straight for the barber's shop to clean up and enjoy a much-needed bath. Then it would be some new duds before hitting the flesh pots.

Laramie Juke had declined to accompany them, so eager was the young cowpoke to hit the tables. Gambling was his weakness and he couldn't wait to get started.

The sour reek of stale sweat and cow dung mingled with cigar smoke in the alcoholic haze. Nobody heeded the newcomer. Just another trail bum eager to spend his hard-earned dough. There were plenty in Dodge more than willing to help him out.

Tossing the set of dice in his right hand, Laramie peered around searching for the craps table. He frowned.

'No dice game operating in here?' he enquired of the rotund bartender.

'The Long Branch only runs poker tables,' the cowboy was briskly informed. 'Try the Saratoga or the Old House down the street aways if'n that's your inclination.'

Juke shrugged. What the heck! Poker would suffice now that he was here. Just sitting at the gambling tables of the famous Long Branch was worth the difference. And he was confident enough to reckon he could hold his own.

'Over here,' called out a snappy dude sporting a red satin vest fronting a flamboyant check shirt. An ace of spades poked from the hatband of a beaverskin derby perched jauntily atop the mat of black hair. 'There's one spare place just a-waiting for a sharp-eyed jasper who wants to make a killing.'

An oily smirk was cemented on to the face of Highspade Jack Daley who was a visiting gambler at the Long Branch. Handing over an agreed proportion of his winnings to the house ensured a

continued residency in the well-frequented saloon.

The game began in a slow, desultory manner. Nobody winning or losing much. That was the way Highspade liked to play it.

Slowly but surely, Juke began to win small but regular amounts which encouraged him to place higher bets. That was when Daley upped the ante.

'How about we raise the limit to fifty bucks?' the gambler suggested, an ingenuous look fixed on his wily visage.

Laramie was all for it, thinking that he had hit on a winning streak. But within a half-hour, the naïve cowpoke had been cleaned out. Right down to his last nickel.

'Seems like Lady Luck ain't helping you out tonight,' mocked Daley. 'Maybe she'll change her mind tomorrow.' The gambler's disdainful guffaw was matched by the other punters who had been much more cautious with their betting. 'That is if'n you can handle a man's game.'

Highspade Daley had realized early

on in the game that the newcomer was not a hardened poker player. He had taken full advantage of that fact.

Laramie ignored the jibe and quickly left the saloon with sniggers of derision spearing his back. He felt humiliated and foolish that he had not had the strength of will to stop when he had the chance. Now he was stony broke.

Once out on the main street he quickly grasped that Dodge City did not welcome those without money to spend. He hadn't even the means to pay for a bed in a flophouse.

Wandering disconsolately down Front Street, he was seriously considering trading in his prized silver pocket watch for some much-needed dough when a sign caught his eye. It was pinned up outside the Woo Ping Chinese Eatery. It read: *Washer-up required immediately. Good pay for right person.*

Juke licked his lips nervously. He peered around to ensure that none of his buddies were in sight. It would not do for a proud cowpuncher like himself

to be found washing dishes, especially in a Chinky dive. But he was broke. Cleaned out on his first day in Dodge City. No wonder the burg had acquired such an infamous reputation. So what choice did he have?

Another quick glance around, then he tore down the sign and stepped through the door. A little man dressed in traditional oriental garb bobbed up to him. The Chinaman bowed three times before asking if the newcomer wanted a table. As soon as Laramie produced the job advertisement, the lackey's manner instantly changed. Gone was the servile humility.

'Umph!' he scoffed. 'Another jumped-up cowboy who has lost all his money.'

Laramie could see that this was clearly a regular means of securing poor saps to engage in the degrading task of kitchen hand. A supercilious thumb ordered the chastened drover to follow him through to the back.

'Another sucker for you, boss,' the waiter informed a man who was supervising the preparation of the food.

Without uttering a word, Woo Ping grabbed an apron and threw it at the newcomer. Then he pointed an arrogant finger towards a growing heap of dirty pots and pans piled high beside a large washing bowl.

Stunned into silence now that the full significance of his plight had been brought home, Laramie just stood there, rooted to the spot, unable to comprehend what his life had become.

The supervisor's face assumed a feral snarl. 'You want job or not?' he shouted in a high-pitched twang that would have been funny in any other circumstances.

Laramie quickly nodded.

'Then you get washing up double quick,' snapped the man as more greasy plates were added to the growing pile. 'And when finished those, always plenty more. Never ending until diner close which not for long time yet.'

Hour after hour Laramie toiled away at the loathsome task. Sweat coursed from every pore of his being. All

sustenance had to be eaten while he was working. There was no let-up for a second. Only when he begged to use the latrine out back was he released from the endless drudgery.

Suddenly at around midnight there was a lull in the endless supply of dirty dishes. But the exhausted dishwasher was given no chance to rest on his laurels. Woo Ping was eager to continue with the torment.

'Go into dining room and clear tables ready for waiters to set up again,' the restaurant owner snapped.

'How much longer before we knock off?' enquired the thoroughly deflated employee.

Ping sniffed. 'Another two hours. So no slacking or wages docked.'

Laramie almost told him to stuff his job where the sun don't shine. But he curbed his restless temper. Such a crazy reaction would forfeit all the money he had already earned. It wasn't much, but every nickel counted when you were in his position.

So the cowpoke lumbered out into the main concourse. He was clearing the tables when five new customers arrived. Laramie gulped. Even with their newly trimmed haircuts, shaved faces and new duds, Wishbone Perry and the other Lazy K hands were unmistakable.

Their faces registered surprise at seeing their erstwhile associate reduced to his current menial status. For a few moments there was silence. Then Clancy Tubb emitted a hoot of scathing laughter. The others quickly joined in.

'Now ain't that something, boys,' hollered Perry, slapping his thigh. 'Old Juke here clearing tables for some Chinky rice-pusher.'

'And he's wearing an apron,' sang out Ten Gallon Charlie Socorro, waving his large hat in the air.

'Maybe he's one of them cross-dressers I been hearing about,' observed a lean jasper known simply as Brewster.

'You figure his real name is Laura and not Laramie?' mocked Wishbone Perry. 'He sure looks like a nancy girl in

that get-up.' This insinuation elicited more sardonic chortling.

But it was left to a raw-boned jasper called Coppernob St John to bring the biting invective to a more serious conclusion.

'Never thought I'd see the day,' he chided with a mystified shake of the head, 'when a fellow puncher would let himself sink to this level. You're a disgrace, Juke. A fella raised in cattle country ought to keep his pride. You're lowering the whole standing of this outfit. When this gets out, the Lazy K will become the joke of the territory. We'll be a laughing stock.' His tone hardened further, bolstered by the amount of liquor they'd all consumed. 'And all on account of your prissy actions.'

That was when things started to get out of hand. Snarls of agreement greeted the assertion. The men pushed forward, eager to teach their Judas associate a hard lesson.

Hearing all this emerging from the mouths of his supposed *compadres* was

too much for Laramie. A dark mask of indignation blurred his reason. He couldn't think straight. First he'd been cleaned out of all his hard-earned pay, then forced to labour at a degrading task, and now he was being insulted by his own kind.

It was all too much.

He flung off the detested apron and dropped his hand to the gun on his hip. But the gun was not there. The others also now realized that they were all unarmed, naked. A feral howl rent the air as Laramie lunged at the nearest man. His grasping hands reached for the guy's throat. Both men went down in a heap of flailing arms and legs.

Laramie came out on top. His hands tightened.

'Get him off'n me!' yelled a terrified Clancy Tubb, 'The guy's crazy.' His face assumed a purple hue. 'Do something afore he kills me.'

That suddenly brought the others back to the reality of their situation. St John, a beefy character over six feet in

height, grabbed Laramie by his collar and heaved him off the wriggling Tubb.

Laramie stumbled across the room, coming to rest beside a table.

'Now let's teach this critter a lesson he'll never forget,' urged Wishbone Perry, who had assumed leadership of the group of vigilantes. They all made to rush the hovering object of their abhorrence.

Laramie grabbed hold of the table and tossed it at the charging cowpokes. Two of them dodged out of the way. But Brewster and Tubb were too slow. The heavy piece of timber struck them both. Tubb absorbed the full force of the table and was knocked out cold. Luckily for Brewster, he was able to fend it off. But his arm was aching something rotten.

St John aimed a solid right hook at Laramie's chin, which he just managed to avoid. But the Coppernob still caught him high up on the forehead. Laramie staggered back, managing to block another haymaker that would

have finished the contest there and then. Spinning on his left heel, Laramie jabbed the other boot heel at his opponent's knee. It connected with a loud thwack.

St John cried in pain as he hopped about on one leg.

Ignoring his buddy's howl of anguish, Perry stepped in and slung a couple of short jabs at Laramie. Both were good solid hits. The young cowboy shook his head, trying to disperse the stunning impact. His eyes glazed over from the hard blows as he backed off to avoid a third punch.

But he wasn't fast enough. Blood spurted from a split lip.

Much as he had given a solid account of himself, Laramie knew that the tide was turning against him.

Out of the corner of his eye Laramie saw a chair hurtling towards him. He cursed knowing that he couldn't have hit St John hard enough. Luckily he managed to duck as the chair soared overhead and crashed into a large

display cabinet. Woo Ping cried out in agonized torment as broken crockery flew everywhere.

Coppernob made a blind rush at his opponent, head down like a charging bull. Laramie just managed to sidestep, allowing the big jasper to thunder past. Chopping down with the rigid side of his hand, he was able to floor the raging redhead.

But there were still three left and they were eager to avenge their fallen comrades.

That was when Laramie was grabbed around the chest from behind. Charlie Socorro had discarded his large hat to reveal a shining bald head. It glistened in the lamplight, seeming to illuminate his fervid intention to maintain a rigid bear-hugging grip on his opponent.

'Slug the bastard while I hold him firm,' he exclaimed, gritting his teeth as Laramie fought back trying to free himself. But his body had been weakened and his efforts were all in vain. Socorro's grip was too strong.

Perry wiped a hand across his mouth. An evil grin signalled his notion that victory was in sight. He pressed forward, fists clenched. Brewster joined him, having armed himself with the leg of a broken chair. He raised it in the fetid air, ready to deliver the *coup de grâce*.

Another panic-stricken holler for them all to stop from Woo Ping went unheeded. Even the threat to summon the marshal had no effect. The blood of the Lazy K avengers was up and only one thing would stay their actions now. Coppernob St John lumbered to his feet. The stocky hulk was eager to rejoin the fray alongside his sidekicks.

But four against one were poor odds, especially for a pinioned body that was unable to protect itself. The assailants moved in, ugly grimaces painted across their faces. Teaching Juke a lesson was going to be easier than taking candy off a kid.

2

A Parting of the Ways

This notion had also entered the thoughtful musings of another customer who had been watching the contest with great interest. The keen-eyed diner had been sitting in a corner minding his own business when the fracas had erupted.

Randy Cavendish was passing through Dodge City on his way west to join his family in Southern Arizona. He had just delivered three prize Brahmin bulls to the Northern Star ranch some five miles east of the city. A letter received only the previous day had come from his father. It was to inform his elder son that he had come into possession of a gold mine in a place called Tascosa Canyon near the town of Jacinto.

According to the elder Cavendish, this one had great potential, and an

extra pair of hands was needed to take full advantage of the family's good fortune.

Randy had smiled at his pa's credulity. How many times did this make it that he had offered his kin the same assurance? It had to be four at least. That was the principal reason why Randy had left to pursue his own path in life elsewhere. Selling cattle had suited his better organized personality.

But now that his business here was complete, Randy was at something of a loose end. A visit to his family after a year away would be a welcome change. He had planned setting out on the long trip to the south-west the following day. That idea was still on the cards. A seat was booked on the morning stagecoach, heading for Santa Fe and beyond.

But first, this guy clearly needed a helping hand.

Randy pushed back his chair. Before the big redhead had the chance to join his buddies, the gatecrasher stepped in to launch a solid straight-armed jab at the cowpoke's head. St John never saw

it coming. His jaw visibly shook under the granite impact. He lurched sideways against a table.

No opportunity was given for St John to recover. Randy grabbed the bullet head and slammed it down on the hard wooden floor.

This unexpected intervention in the crew's plan of retribution caused Socorro to loosen his hold on the captive. Laramie sensed a turn in his fortunes. Jamming his bootheel into the guy's shin, he slammed his head back, connecting with Socorro's blue-veined snout. A yowl of agony accompanied the loosening of his grip, enabling Laramie to break free of the stifling bear-hug.

'Yaroooo!' howled Socorro, lurching back and holding his bleeding proboscis. 'The bastard's done broken my nose.'

Laramie took full advantage of his good fortune. A quick turn and two short jabs drove the hollering puncher backwards. Woo Ping joined in by laying him out with a frying pan. The Chinaman trilled with excitement.

Now it was two against two. Much better odds for a gambling man.

Laramie threw a smile of thanks at his saviour. The pair squared their shoulders hunkering down ready to tackle the remaining aggressors.

In the blink of an eye the situation had changed. Sensing that it was now or never, Wishbone Perry uttered a brutish growl of rage and bulldozed wildly at the intruder. But Laramie's benefactor deftly stepped to one side and slugged him with a heavy iron coffee pot. That put Perry out of action.

Brewster was now the only one left on his feet.

Observing that the rabble's bullying advantage had been clearly lost, due to the stranger's intervention, he quickly backed off. The fight was over.

'OK, you win,' he wailed, throwing down the chair leg and raising his hands in surrender. 'We've had enough.'

After helping his stricken comrades to their feet Brewster retreated towards the door.

Laramie and the Good Samaritan stood side by side amidst the wreckage of the Chinese restaurant. Breathing heavily, they watched stony-faced as the beaten cowpokes made to depart.

But it was too late.

Filling out a smart black suit, a bulky jasper stood in the open door of the eatery. A shotgun was clasped in one hand, a six-gun in the other. The tin star pinned to his vest confirmed the arrival of the law. Marshal Earp's drooping moustache twitched. Hovering behind him was the jittery restaurant owner's assistant, who had been dispatched for help.

One of the Loomis barrels exploded in a blast of smoke and buckshot. Plaster drifted down from the ceiling, where a ragged hole had appeared.

'Anybody moves a muscle,' growled a low yet imposing voice, 'and they get the other barrel up their ass.' A look that brooked no dissention glued the perpetrators to the spot. Earp's probing eye scanned the smashed-up room. Satisfied that he was in full control, the

lawman snapped, 'Against that wall, the lot of you.'

No argument was forthcoming. Wyatt Earp had that effect on men. The brusque command included everyone, as well as Laramie and his rescuer. There were no winners and losers as far as the lawman was concerned — except for himself, of course.

'So what happened here?' the marshal demanded of no one in particular. It was Randy Cavendish who offered a concise yet accurate description of the recent events.

'That right, Ping?' Earp enquired of the restaurant owner.

But the Chinaman was not so certain.

'Dishwasher was insulted but he should have been more accepting, honoured sir,' warbled the jumpy oriental, his black pigtail bouncing up and down like a jack-in-the-box. 'Customer always right is good Chinese proverb.' He was thinking that it was his employee's fault that the premises had been trashed.

But Wyatt Earp was a true frontiersman. An insult such as had been dished out here needed challenging. And five against one was not a praiseworthy contest. He was, therefore, inclined to concur with the man who had stepped in to help, and he made sure that the Chinaman knew it.

Ping conceded, promising not to dock Laramie's wages. That was when another man arrived on the scene. Ira Kemp had been heading back to the hotel when he heard the ruckus. Seeing that his men were involved, he hurried across.

'What in thunder is going on here, Copper?' he bawled at his dishevelled ramrod.

The cowpoke reddened with awkwardness.

'Sorry, boss,' whined the hefty cowpoke. 'It were this critter that — '

Before he could try to wheedle out of the responsibility that rested on his shoulders, Cavendish butted in to apprise the newcomer of the full story.

Kemp's face took on a look of intense fury. As his complexion assumed shades of purple, lilac and red, he blustered and spat before hauling off a full invective against his men.

At last, as Kemp drew breath following the vehement diatribe, Woo Ping stepped in with his ten dollars' worth. 'Who pay for damage?' he tweeted like a frightened canary.

'Send me the bill,' growled Kemp. 'And I'll be making darned sure that every last cent comes out of their wages until it's been paid off.' Then, with a final wave of dismissal, he addressed the marshal. 'That OK with you, Wyatt?'

'Guess so, Ira,' the lawman replied, keeping his gun levelled. 'But make certain these varmints head straight back to camp. I see any of them on Front Street again this season, I'll lock 'em up and throw away the key.'

With that he left and the party dispersed, leaving Woo Ping and his employees to clear up the mess. Randy offered his help in order to speed things

up. The Chinaman was exceedingly grateful and refused payment for his meal.

A half-hour later, with money in his pocket once again, Laramie Juke and his new buddy were enjoying a quiet drink in the Occidental saloon, where Randy was staying.

Located at the end of Front Street adjoining the schoolhouse, it offered a less hectic environment, and the guest bedrooms were of a superior quality. It was not exactly placid and tranquil like the premises on the far side of the railroad track, where the regular citizens lived, but preferable to the rowdy hallooing around the Long Branch.

'I owe you a lot for helping me out,' Laramie professed with gratitude to his companion as he imbibed a much-needed mouthful of cold beer. 'If'n you hadn't barged in, them guys would have beaten me to a pulp.'

'That's what too much of this stuff does to a man,' his buddy agreed, jabbing a finger at his own glass.

Laramie rubbed his jaw wincing at the tenderness. 'Guess I did let the side down though.' He sighed wistfully. 'Can't rightly blame the boys. But a man needs dough in a place like this. And washing dishes was my only chance.' Again the puncher shook his head with self-reproach. 'It's the gambling that always gets me into bother. In future I'm gonna stick with craps and leave the cards alone.'

Randy couldn't resist a chuckle at the dubious logic expressed by his associate.

'Where did you lose all your money?'

'In the Long Branch,' came back the morose reply, 'to a smarmy dude with an ace of pips stuck in his hat.'

Randy sucked in his lips. 'Man!' he exclaimed, 'if'n I'd known earlier, I could have saved you being taken for a ride.'

'What do you mean? I couldn't spot any kind of double-dealing. Far as I could tell, he won fair and square.'

'That's because craps is your game,'

Randy told him. 'In future leave the cards to those that know them. That guy is a regular tinhorn. He comes to Dodge every summer just to prey on cowpokes eager for a good time.'

'Too late now to do anything about it,' Laramie moaned, finishing off his drink.

'Not if'n we head down to the Long Branch straight away,' enthused Randy, getting to his feet. 'We could catch the bastard and force his hand.'

Hurrying off down the street, they could hear the Dodge City Band pounding out a popular tune in the saloon's dance hall.

However, they were out of luck in their primary quest. Highspade Daley was nowhere in sight. Another dealer had taken his place. On being questioned, the 'keep informed them that the gambler had left town soon after his last game had finished.

'That was over two hours ago,' the barman said, polishing a glass.

'Which way was he headed?' asked

Randy impatiently.

The barman shrugged apathetically, turning away to serve another customer.

'He could have gone in any one of four directions from here,' mused Randy. 'Ain't no way we can trail him in the dark.'

'And by morning he could be any place,' added a downcast Laramie Juke, one shoulder lifting in reluctant acceptance that his dough was well and truly gone. 'Guess that's that, then. At least now I know to stick to craps in future.'

They wandered back to the Occidental. Randy had managed to secure his new associate a room in the saloon. The manager only agreed after the new patron took a much-needed bath. Some deft scissor work by Randy plus a loan of his cut-throat razor gave Laramie Juke a whole different appearance.

Laramie was up at first light. He wanted to catch Ira Kemp before the rancher left on the long ride back to Texas. Luckily, the cowboy's skills in cutting and branding were much valued by the

astute rancher. However, a stern lecture was delivered on the pitfalls of gambling, although the Lazy K boss recognized that Wishbone Perry and his cronies were to blame for the previous night's brawl.

Following a hearty breakfast in the Occidental dining room, the two buddies parted company. Each man promised to keep in touch with the other. Although how that would be possible in the wide open territories of the expanding Western frontier was anybody's guess.

'You can always contact me at the Lazy K down in the Brazos country,' Laramie stated as they strolled down to the Butterfield depot. 'The boss has kept me on, so I'll be heading south later today.'

They shook hands through the open window of the stagecoach as it was pulling out, neither knowing when, if at all, they would meet up again. Little did they suspect the circumstances in which their next encounter would be played out.

3

Paydirt

All was quiet in Tascosa Canyon. Only the lyrical chirping of a cactus wren disturbed the tranquil calm.

The hot noonday sun had sucked every last globule of moisture from the bare orange sandstone walls that loomed over the narrow fissure. But all was not as desolate as appeared at a first glance in this remote outpost.

Various strains of vegetation had somehow managed to adapt to the harsh, arid environment. Most common were the twisted branches of mesquite intermingled with the ubiquitous salt-bush. Adding some vibrant colour were cream stands of teddy bear cholla cacti.

And, following the rare flash storm of the night before, red poppies could be seen waving their elegant stems in the

low after-breeze.

At the far end of the canyon stood a solitary cabin. Constructed from plank wood brought in by wagon, it was home to Bendigo Cavendish and his family.

Ever since his Uncle George had hightailed it for California in the '49 gold rush and brought back exciting tales of fortunes made and lost, Ben had been hooked on searching out the elusive yellow metal. As soon as he was old enough, the young man hit the trail for Virginia City in Utah to try his luck on the legendary Comstock Lode.

The story of how Henry Comstock made his discovery was often told around camp fires. Back in the 1850s Comstock had happened upon some greenhorn miners. The poor saps had failed to appreciate the richness of the vein upon which they had stumbled. Taking advantage of their ignorance, the silver-tongued prospector immediately staked his own claim to the land. And along with some partners, he began working it.

Rumours abounded that Old Pancake, as he was known, bought out one guy's share for a bottle of whiskey and a blind horse. The astute prospector must surely have realized early on that he had acquired one of the richest sources of gold and silver ever found.

After hearing about Comstock's lucky break Ben Cavendish, like thousands of his contemporaries, was well and truly hooked. After staking his own claim, he was fortunate enough to dig out sufficient paydirt from the ground to whet his appetite for more. But he was never to be as fortunate as Old Pancake.

Loneliness was always a frequent companion to prospectors.

Women were understandably in short supply in the gold camps. Apart, that was, from the swarms of calico queens who descended on such dens of iniquity to help the prospectors spend their hard-won lucre. The only way for a man to acquire a female partner was from a lonely hearts catalogue.

So that is what Ben Cavendish did.

After getting married he tried to please his new bride by settling down to a mundane life raising chickens. But it was always going to be a losing battle. He stuck to the grinding drudgery for four miserable years. But that was enough. Ben couldn't resist chasing after the next gold strike that caught his fancy.

Marcia Cavendish realized her mistake in getting hitched to such a man. She promptly left their three children with a neighbour before disappearing back East. From that day, when the siblings were only knee-high to a grasshopper, they had accompanied their father on all his expeditions.

The gold-bearing ore had been found in sufficient quantities to keep body and soul together. But no real strike of any consequence had thus far been made. The elder of the Cavendish boys had tired of the endless quest. Cutting loose, Randy had headed for Kansas, where the booming cattle industry

offered more stable employment.

That left Ben with his younger son and his daughter who arrived in Tascosa Canyon during the spring of 1877.

Three months had passed since the family had arrived in the canyon. So far, they had made steady yet uninspiring progress. Even with the extra help of Randy following his return from Kansas, no big finds had been made.

Shona Cavendish was busy shovelling gravel into a log flume. The sluice pursued a meandering course from the upper section of Catalina Creek down to where the gravel was sifted. Shona was a trim young woman. The rough denim jeans, faded check shirt and battered Stetson meant that from a distance she could easily pass for a man. It was only on closer acquaintance that it became patently obvious that she was a comely female with curves in all the right places.

She had steadfastly refused to accept the normal domestic routine expected of frontier women. In consequence, all such chores were shared out equally

between her father and brothers.

Today was Pa's turn for cooking the meals. Not a choice to stimulate the taste buds. Golden locks tied back in a pony tail peeped from under the wide brim of her hat as Shona assiduously applied herself to the demanding labour.

Downstream, beside the exit of the flume, her elder brother Randy was idly checking the riffles for any sign of the elusive glint.

He was beginning to understand why the previous tenant had abandoned the claim.

'Won't pay you nought but nickels and dimes,' the old reprobate had asserted with a chuckle as he led his fully laden burro off in search of the next big strike.

But Ben was convinced that Raccoon Micah Phelps had been digging in the wrong place. All the signs on the opposite side of the canyon pointed to this being ideal terrain for rich pickings. So far, however, it appeared that Raccoon

had been correct in his assessment.

Until now.

Randy Cavendish was about to throw a stone at a nosy desert rat when his eye was caught by a sharp glint in the riffle box. Quickly he discarded the stone, fingers eagerly clawing at the heap of loose gravel. Then he saw it. Not one but three nuggets of gold shining brightly. More twinkling gleams like elusive fish in a pond caught his attention.

The young man grabbed up the largest specimen. His voracious eyes eagerly devoured the iridescent beauty of the rough-hewn chunk. His mouth hung open, lips flapping impotently, such was the shock of the discovery. At last he found his voice.

'Hey, Brad!' he called to his younger brother, who was further down by the creek testing out a gold-filtering rocker-box he had built. 'Come over here and take a look at this.'

Bradley Cavendish paused and looked up. Seeing his brother's frantic wave, he hurried over. As soon as his eyes locked

on to the glittering chunks, he gave vent to a boisterous howl of elation.

'Gold! Gold!' he yelled for all to hear. 'We've finally struck it rich!'

Quickly the two brothers removed the nuggets. Their father was just emerging from the cabin, covered in flour. The raucous holler had easily penetrated the thin walls.

'You ain't jokin', are yuh, boy?' Ben huffed, unable to believe that his predictions had come true at last.

'Just take a look at this beauty, Pa,' Randy spluttered, his voice trilling with excitement. 'I ain't never seen nothing like it before. And there's more to come.' His finger jabbed as another hefty nugget rolled down on to the strip of carpet lining the end of the riffle.

Ben threw off his apron and hurried down to the creek to join his animated son.

A grin wider than the Mississippi in flood spread across his face.

'Didn't I say that coming to Tascosa Canyon was gonna be our lucky break?'

He picked up one of the nuggets. 'And this little sparkler proves I was right.'

Her brother's strident call had reached Shona's ears higher up the canyon. Unable to catch the wording, she nonetheless picked up on the urgency of his summons. Abandoning her gruelling chore, Shona rushed headlong down the narrow trail.

'Ain't that the purtiest thing you ever did see, gal?' Ben gushed, holding up the nugget for the sunlight to play across its gnarled profile.

'Sure is, Pa,' interjected Shona staring at the knobbly lump of rock. 'It makes all this hard graft worthwhile.' Her eyes glazed over as visions of fine dresses and servants tending to her every whim swam into focus.

Ever the practical one, Randy voiced a concern that the suddenness of the discovery had pasted over. 'Let's hope it's a proper seam and not just some odd bits that have been washed downstream from old Raccoon's abandoned diggings.'

'You're right, boy,' agreed his father. 'We need to check the adit to see if'n we've done hit the mother lode.'

A mood of restrained tension settled over the Cavendish family as they hustled back up to the entrance to the mine level. Above the dark opening was a sign announcing the name of the holding — *El Dorado*. They could only hope and pray that the Spanish name held true.

All thoughts of a meal were forgotten. The lure of gold and the need to ascertain the value of their find overshadowed everything else.

'You kids wait out here while I check it out,' Ben ordered his kin.

Taking a lighted torch, he ventured into the Stygian gloom of the mine entrance. So far, they had tunnelled into the depths of the Dragoon Mountains for a distance of half a mile. Much of the narrow passageway was supported by wooden beams. On the floor, wooden rails had been laid down on which stood a handcart to carry out

the gold-bearing rock and gravel.

A frustrating hour of hanging around on tenterhooks followed before Ben Cavendish emerged. The look on his leathery face gave nothing away. Only when a beaming smile revealed teeth yellowed by baccy-chewing did the others know that they had indeed struck *el Dorado*.

'This is it.' Ben's voice emerged barely above a whisper, a hoarse croak filled with emotion. 'This is the one strike for which I been searching all my life.' His eyes filled as tears brimmed over.

Shona laid a comforting arm around her father's shoulder. 'If'n anybody deserves the attentions of Lady Luck, then it's you, Pa,' she enthused.

'Sooner we can register this claim with the county assay office the better,' Randy cautioned, once again bringing their attention back to the hard realities of their situation. 'Until that's done and we have an official certificate giving us the right to mine here, any darned claim-jumper can muscle in and take

over our holding.'

'Any jasper tries muscling in around here and he'll get a bellyful of lead.' Brad drew his latest acquisition, a new .45 revolver with nickel-plated finish. It was his pride and joy. The young hothead twirled the gun on his middle finger, demonstrating his prowess with evident satisfaction.

'Put that darned thing away,' snapped his father. 'While I'm in charge, there'll be no gunplay unless we're threatened.'

Brad obeyed with reluctance.

Satisfied that his authority had been maintained, Ben went on, 'Randy's hit the nail on the head, though.' The possibility that anybody could threaten their holding had brought him down to earth concerning the legal rights of prospecting. 'One of us must go to Tucson and get it sorted out.'

Before they could discuss the matter further Shona's elegant nose sniffed the air. 'What's that smell of burning?' she enquired, a worried frown clouding her dirt-smeared features.

'I'd say it's that deer stew Pa's been working on all morning,' replied Brad, once again his affable self.

The gold discovery had driven all thoughts of food from their minds. Now suddenly they felt ravenously hungry.

'Sorry, kids.' Ben lifted his shoulders in a shrug of apology. 'Looks like we'll have to make do with sourdough bread and refried beans again.'

'This time I reckon it's gonna taste like prime rib steak with all the trimmings.'

They all laughed gleefully at Randy's blithe remark as the tension brought about by their lucrative find drained away.

After much deliberation it was decided that Ben was the best person to head for the territorial centre of Tucson to make that all-important claim registration. Being the head of the family, his signature would be needed to legitimize the venture.

It was a three-day ride, so he could expect to be away for a week at the

most. In the meantime, Shona and Randy would continue the excavation ready for registering the claim at the local assay office in Jacinto.

The journey to Tucson lay north-west across rough terrain dominated by the giant Saguaro cacti. These towering organ pipes with their thick green arms characterize this part of the Sonora desert in southern Arizona. Some of the mighty sentinels grow to fifty feet in height and are over one hundred years old. Their white flowers light up the harsh arid terrain in late spring.

Ben Cavendish loved the wild solitude of the desert, which always imbued him with a sense of tranquillity. But on this occasion while following the narrow trail his thoughts were elsewhere.

One hand continually strayed to the saddle-bag in which were secreted samples of the newly discovered gold seam. He could only hope that the ore was rich enough to warrant an extension of the mine working. It would be a costly undertaking, eating up much of

their savings. But well worth the expense and effort if there was sufficient gold to extract from *El Dorado*.

★　★　★

Tucson was a rip-roaring boom town in full swing.

The name stems from the Papago Indian word meaning *settlement near black-based mountain*. The mountain in question is the Sentinel which once acted as a lookout post when Indians held sway before the invading pioneers drove them out. By 1877, however, gold prospectors dominated the streets of the thriving settlement.

The territorial assay office lay half-way down Sonora Street on the right. Although hungry and tired from his gruelling trek, Ben wasted no time in idle speculation. He would only be able to rest easy once the value of the claim was verified and his ownership endorsed in writing.

On entering the office he immediately

noticed that the place was neat and tidy. Everything in its rightful place. Pictures of successful mining dignitaries hung on the flock-papered walls. There was none of the jumbled clutter associated with most frontier establishments.

The man standing behind the counter was no sourdough miner. He sported a dark store-bought suit with a crisp white shirt and black necktie. Jethro Pucket exuded a haughty arrogance designed to instil diffidence into those who frequented such premises. Unknown to his clients Pucket always stood on a box to gain extra height. It gave him an added measure of superiority.

Ben was used to dealing with such overbearing turnips. Nonetheless, he still felt decidedly scruffy in these opulent surroundings.

'Can I help you, sir?' enquired the puffed-up clerk.

'I want this sample testing for its gold content,' the visitor replied, indicating the sack of rocks. 'No sense in continuing to work the diggings if'n it ain't

worth the effort.'

'There is a ten dollar fee for that service,' said the clerk, holding out his hand. 'You can collect the report in the morning before deciding whether to register the claim.'

Ben handed over the fee. Much to the clerk's annoyance, he hefted the heavy bag containing his samples on to the highly polished counter.

'Over there on that bench, if you please,' rapped an indignant Pucket.

'Sorry about that,' muttered the customer, shifting the bag. Then, with a half-hearted attempt at levity, he asked, 'Mind pointing me in the direction of a decent eating house? My stomach's clucking worse than a turkey at Thanksgiving.'

The clerk was not amused as he vigorously buffed the counter. His beaky snout twitched with distaste as he peered over his steel-rimmed pince-nez. 'Try the Miner's Hash House down the street.'

Such a down-at-heel place was clearly good enough for this tramp, and with

that, he dismissed the ageing prospector and returned to studying his ledger.

Ben shrugged. He aimed a silent grimace towards the bald-headed weasel as he made to leave the assay office. As it turned out, the suggested eatery was far more to his liking than any stuck-up restaurant. Basic fare and plenty of it, washed down with hot strong coffee.

The next morning when he faced the vainglorious Jethro Pucket, Ben's nerves were in a tangled knot of anxiety. Butterflies fluttered in his stomach. His grey beard itched something terrible and he was hard put not to scratch at it.

How had the assessment gone? Was it the rich ore on which he was banking, or just a misplaced anomaly?

Pucket was all smiles. Ben sighed with relief. No longer the imperious toad of the previous afternoon, the land agent was now a fawning minion. Pudgy hands rubbed together as he bowed with an unctuous smile before such a distinguished client.

'It would appear, Mr Cavendish, that

your sample is one of the richest in the territory. Indeed, the Land Agency has never come across gold content as high as this. Can I ask where it is located?'

'South-east of here in Tascosa Canyon, near the town of Jacinto,' Ben gushed. This was far better than he could ever have expected. His whole body relaxed. The tight strain of the last few days dissipated in a vibe of animated euphoria. The next half-hour was spent in a daze, filling in forms.

Finally, still in a dreamlike trance, he signed the certificate of authenticity. Sanctioned with the company's red seal, it stated that he now had the full and legal right to mine the land in the designated locality and keep the profits acquired thereon, subject to a land survey to determine the physical extent of the claim.

It was a stirring moment as he wandered out of the office.

'One more thing,' the now-grovelling clerk called after him. Ben paused in the doorway. 'You would be advised to

take care when dealing with the authorities in Jacinto. We have received suspect reports concerning the activities of Mayor Daley and his associates.'

If the preoccupied miner took heed of the warning he gave no indication. His whole attention was focused on absorbing the swanky document. Reverently he slid the parchment back into its folder and mounted up.

Pucket shrugged as the miner spurred off. Then he quickly forgot about his previous client, turning instead to deal with yet another dishevelled gold-hungry patron hovering by the door of his office.

4

Incident in Tascosa Canyon

The next prescribed task was to register the claim in Jacinto so that the agent there could assess the full extent of the land being worked. Only a short deviation was needed to get the ball rolling. So one week after departing from Tascosa Canyon, Ben Cavendish found himself entering yet another assay office.

He was lucky that Specs Reisling was free to accompany him straight back to the mine. On hearing the assay result, confirming the rich vein of gold-bearing ore, Shona and Randy were over the moon. As it was getting late in the day Reisling set to work immediately.

'I'll need to carry out a full survey to determine the extent of your claim,' he informed the exhilarated miners. 'With all the measurements in hand I will

then be able to draw up a plan of your holding for the written contract.'

'Will that make the mine legally ours?' Shona asked.

'Sure will, miss,' the agent assured her, making his way across to the entrance. 'And the sooner I get started the better, wouldn't you say?'

'Not even time for a cup of coffee and one of Shona's apple turnovers?' Full of bonhomie, Randy aimed a beaming grin at the agent.

Reisling pushed the thick lenses that had given him his nickname up his nose. It was a long time since lunch and his stomach was rumbling. 'Www-weeeelll now!' he drawled out, licking his lips. 'Maybe I could spare a few minutes to appease this guy.' He tapped a rotund belly that had draped its substantial girth over his belt.

Ten minutes later, having sunk three cups of coffee and an equal number of cakes, he disappeared into the depths of the mine.

When he had departed Ben suddenly

cottoned to the fact that his younger son was absent. 'Where's Brad?' he asked.

'He took the wagon down to the Coronado woodyard for those extra pit props and angle iron supports that we'll be needing,' replied Shona.

Ben nodded. 'All this extra gear will take most of what we've salted away now that our claim is moving into the big time.'

The land agent was gone for some fifty minutes.

Outside the mine entrance the Cavendish clan could only wait and trust that the inspection would be positive. Randy paced up and down busily smoking one quirly after another. Their father whittled away at a piece of wood. Only Shona remained calm and unaffected by the tense atmosphere.

After what seemed like a lifetime, Reisling reappeared.

'Everything in order, Specs?' enquired Ben, striving to hide the nervous croak with a brief cough.

'Don't foresee any problems,' replied the land agent, stuffing his papers and measuring equipment back into a saddle-bag. Mounting his horse he said, 'Drop by the office in a few days and I'll have the deeds ready for collection.'

Had the prospective mine owners been more observant they might have questioned why Reisling was so anxious to leave. The setting sun hadn't yet disappeared over the crest of the Dragoons. The much-enjoyed extra cakes that Shona had promised to give him for his wife were completely forgotten. A nervous tic that would surely have raised eyebrows was hidden behind the thick glass of the agent's spectacles.

But the miners were too cock-a-hoop about their new venture to bother with incidentals. Exchanging cheery waves the surveyor spurred off back towards Jacinto.

The agent's blotchy features no longer wore his previously affable mood. Specs Reisling had made a discovery inside the mine that was disconcerting to say

the least. And it had nothing to do with any misapprehensions regarding the richness of the gold seam.

★ ★ ★

Highspade Jack Daley was sampling his latest batch of single malt Scotch whiskey specially imported from a supplier in Kansas City. He had been Mayor of Jacinto for six months and now had the town running according to his tune. Daley believed in dressing to suit his position. He had acquired his strange nickname in Dodge City, where he had been a professional gambler.

An ace of spades stuck in his pearl-grey hatband had become a trademark. But gone were the garish duds he had favoured as a gambler. The new Stetson was offset by a smart powder-blue three-piece suit with ruffled white shirt and red cravat sporting a diamond stickpin. His thick black hair was slicked back and neatly trimmed, his waxed moustache slightly curled at the ends.

The mayor and his officials occupied a purpose-built office in the middle of town. It dominated the plaza and had been one of the first projects of the new mayor following his election. No expense had been spared to accord the new bureaucrat all the trappings of his high status in the community.

Needless to say, rents had gone up sharply to pay for the extravagance. One storekeeper who had complained suddenly found his premises mysteriously being consumed by fire when he arrived the next morning. That had quickly brought all the other tradespeople into line.

The mayor lit up a large Cuban cigar. Casually allowing the blue smoke to dribble from between thin lips he addressed his confederate.

Hymie Weiss was a lawyer on Daley's payroll. It was his job to make sure all transactions effected by the mayor, however dubious and underhand, were within the letter of the law if not its morality.

'Any problems with those rent rises

we sent out last week?' Daley enquired.

'A few moans and groans, which was to be expected.' Weiss accepted a glass of whiskey. 'Only fly in the ointment is that tetchy spinster who runs the dressmaker's. Caused a right old hoohah when I gave her the new lease to sign.' The lawyer balked at the memory of a young and attractive woman castigating him and his two hard-assed bodyguards.

Leaning back in his seat, Highspade planted his polished boots on the desk top and considered the problem. No darned shopkeeper, especially a woman, was going to thwart his money-making schemes. 'Maybe if'n I send the boys round to rough her place up, it'll make the dame see sense?'

'Nothing too obvious, Jack,' chided his associate, wagging a cautionary finger. 'We can't afford to get on the wrong side of the law with you intending to run for county commissioner.'

The mayor nodded. 'Guess you're right there, Hymie. Let me think on it a spell.'

At that moment a knock sounded on the door of the plush upstairs office. Highspade frowned. He wasn't expecting anybody. And his secretary downstairs had been given instructions that he was not to be disturbed.

'Who is it?' he called out gruffly.

'It's me, Mr Mayor, Specs Reisling — '

'Come back in an hour,' the bristling Mayor interrupted. 'I'm busy.'

'I've found out something that you'll want to hear,' the land surveyor stressed, 'and it could make you the richest guy in the territory.'

A brief silence followed as Highspade considered this startling announcement. The mayor threw a bemused look at his associate. Weiss shrugged. This wasn't his decision to make.

'OK,' the mayor replied after due deliberation. 'Come on in. But whatever's eating you, it better be good.'

Specs entered the opulent room, removing his hat. 'You said that I should inform you immediately if'n a claim was registered. Well, not only is this a big daddy,

more to the point . . . ' Specs hesitated, seeing that he now had the mayor's complete attention. He cast a wary eye towards the hovering lawyer, who was likewise curious as to this unexpected assertion.

'Go on then!' blustered Daley, eager to hear what the little runt had to say. 'What's so darned special about it?' Then he noticed the agent nervously glancing towards the other man. 'And don't be worrying about Hymie, he's one of the boys.'

Satisfied, Reisling launched into the details of his discovery.

'I've just finished a survey of the Cavendish mine out at Tascosa Canyon. The gold seam they've hit upon has its origins on your property on the far side of the canyon. If'n my memory serves me correct, there's some law stating that as a consequence, you own the rights to all the ore dug out.'

The shifty informant waited a moment to allow his discovery to sink in before continuing. He was not disappointed.

Daley's eyes had lit up.

'I've seen the county commissioner's mining authorization. Believe me, Mr Mayor, when I say that in all my experience in this business, I ain't never come across a richer strike in the whole of Arizona.'

'Let me get this straight,' said Daley, enunciating every syllable. 'You're saying that all the gold being mined in Tascosa Canyon is mine?'

'That's the durned truth,' Reisling stressed with a grin.

'I'm much obliged to you, Specs, for letting me know about this,' said the mayor handing over a cigar and lighting it for the surveyor. 'And I'll see to it that there's a bonus for you at the end of the month.'

Reisling was only one of numerous people in Jacinto on the mayor's illicit payroll. Acquiring information about all manner of dealings had been essential in Jack Daley's rise to the position of power and influence that he now commanded. He turned away effectively

terminating the discussion.

When the little guy had departed Daley turned to his colleague. 'Have you heard about this decree?'

Weiss nodded, adding, 'One thing he didn't mention, though, was that there's an occupation clause to make it effective.'

'What does that mean?'

'You need to have been the owner of the land where the motherlode has its source for a full twelve-month period, otherwise it ceases to apply.' The lawyer fixed his associate with a guarded look. 'How long have you owned that piece of land, Jack?'

Daley remained tight-lipped. His silence spoke volumes.

'Well, it sure ain't that long,' eventually came back the terse retort. 'But we keep that piece of information strictly to ourselves. You got me?'

'Sure, sure,' iterated Weiss puffing casually on his cigar. 'Of course, now that I have to . . . shall we say . . . suppress what I know when drawing up the document of rights, it's going to cost a sight

more than normal.'

Daley stiffened. He recognized a shakedown when he saw one. But there was nothing he could do about it. For the moment, that was.

The crooked lawyer was not intimidated by the glowering stare. He knew that he had the upper hand. He was going to make certain that he profited from this unexpected windfall. 'I'll get things moving straight away. We don't want to waste any time in the important business of making us both rich men, do we?'

Daley responded with a curt nod as the lawyer moved across to the door. The deceitful smile pasted across the mayor's face gave no hint of the menacing thoughts whirling round inside his head.

As soon as the door closed his features warped into a twisted grimace of anger. He needed Weiss to ensure that the *El Dorado* mine became his property. The law would have to be bent to accommodate that eventuality.

But once he became the legal title-holder, Hymie Weiss would become surplus to requirements. Then there would be nobody to challenge that entitlement.

★ ★ ★

It was early morning in Tascosa Canyon.

The Cavendish crew had already been at work for two hours. In truth, they should have waited until the land surveyor had delivered their official mining lease. But there was no reason to suppose that any problems would arise. So they had continued, with Ben drawing up a list of special equipment that would be required to reap the full benefit of their bonanza.

The older man was sitting at the table scribbling down calculations regarding costs when he heard the sound of approaching horses echoing along the enclosed canyon. Ever the cautious operator, Ben grabbed up his old Spencer rifle and

moved out on to the veranda of the cabin.

The group of five riders were headed by the sheriff.

Wes Tomlin drew his mount to a thundering halt in a cloud of dust outside the cabin. The tin star glinted in the sunlight. The other riders all wore the official insignia of deputies. Their boisterous arrival was meant to intimidate the mine owner. But Cavendish stood his ground, giving no hint that the ploy had achieved its aim. Straight away he had picked up on the hostile mood of the visitors.

A mirthless smile cracked the miner's craggy visage. 'To what do we owe this unexpected call, Sheriff?' he enquired, keeping a firm grip on the rifle.

Without any preamble, Tomlin got straight down to business.

'This ain't no social call,' the lawman rasped. He extracted an envelope from his pocket and handed it to Cavendish. 'My orders are to wait for a reply, so you best read it straight away.'

Intrigued, the mine owner stepped down and accepted the proffered letter. Quickly backing off, he said, 'You can water your mounts down by the creek while I see what this is all about.' Without waiting for a reply or offering the riders any refreshment, he re-entered the cabin.

'What did those men want?' Shona asked, wiping her floured hands on a cloth.

'A letter here from the town lawyer.' For a full minute Ben Cavendish stared at the official envelope, a frown darkening his expression. 'I got me a bad feeling about this,' he murmured.

'Let's see what it says before you get all down in the mouth,' Shona pressed her father. 'It might be good news about the claim.'

'That durned tinstar didn't give that impression.'

Ben slit open the envelope, extracted the sheet and slowly read its contents. And it soon became clear that Ben's cynical mood had been well founded.

'What does it say?' enquired his concerned daughter.

'According to a county ruling dug out by a lawyer in Jacinto, we don't own the rights to any gold extracted from the mine after all.' Ben threw the damning missive down on to the table. 'It all belongs to that toad of a mayor, Jack Daley.'

'How do they make that out?' exclaimed Shona, grabbing the letter and quickly scanning the spidery handwriting. She released a stream of unladylike expletives before spitting out, 'And the rat has given us a week to comply before he takes control of the mine.'

Father and daughter could only sit there, stunned into silence by this catastrophic news. Suddenly, all their dreams of success and a life of ease had been thrown into disarray. And all because of some obscure edict.

'It's not fair!' Shona blurted out, tears streaming down her face. 'This is our claim and nobody should have the right to take it from us like this. The

price that chiseller has offered would be laughable if it wasn't so insulting.'

Ben snarled out his own brand of exasperation. 'You're right, girl. Ain't no way that I'm handing over this claim to any damned town lackey for a pittance. I'd rather go down fighting than submit to a scheming racket like this.'

At that moment a raucous shout from outside broke into their furious exchange.

'You best come out and give me your answer, Cavendish,' growled the sheriff. 'I ain't got all day to hang around here.'

'Then what are we waiting for?' snapped Ben's daughter, scrambling to her feet. 'Let's be giving these turkeys a taste of what to expect if'n they are thinking to take over the *El Dorado* by force.'

Father and daughter hustled outside, their guns clearly on show.

'You can tell your boss that he can go roast his butt in hell!' Shona howled indignantly. 'We'll fight anyone who tries to run us off our claim with some

trumped-up piece of wordplay.'

'And is that your decision as well, mister?' enquired Tomlin.

Before Cavendish had the chance to reply, a hard-nosed *hombre* sporting a black patch pushed his way through from the back of the group.

One-eyed Digger Brown was of Australian origin. He had stowed away on a ship bound for California after killing a gold prospector for his poke. The guy had not gone down without a fight, which left Brown looking at the world through a single peeper. The killer's cavalier disposition had likewise suffered, leaving him tetchy and irascible.

The dubious deputy now pinned the speaker down with his good eye, a rasping drawl responding to the girl's snarled declaration.

'A yellow rat that hides behind a woman's skirts don't deserve no second chance.' Brown slapped leather. 'I say we get the job done here and now to save time.'

There was a murmur of agreement from the other deputies as they pushed forward to back up Digger Brown's confrontation.

'And we can have us some fun at the same time,' sniggered a thin-faced jasper leering heavily at the shapely contours beneath the girl's work clothes.

Coarse chortles accompanied this suggestion from Kid Mancos.

The sheriff was taken by surprise. Daley's pawn, he had only accepted the job two weeks previously following the shooting of the last incumbent.

Colorado Tod Benson had refused to do the bidding of the mayor and had paid the ultimate price. The verdict stated that he had been shot in the back by person or persons unknown. Tomlin's authority was shaky at best. Now under pressure for the first time, he had neither the will nor fortitude to resist.

But help was at hand from an unlikely source. It came from another voice, strong and forceful, that halted any precipitate action on the part of the

posse. The challenge emanated from the entrance to the mine.

'Any man draws a gun and I'll drill him clean through the head,' came the vigorous response to the one-eyed ruffian's threat. To show that he meant business, Randy Cavendish dispatched a bullet that lifted Brown's hat into the air. Another sent it spinning off into a bush. 'And my pa and sister are just as good with their hoglegs.'

The impressive display of trigger-nometry was effective. Those members of the posse who had favoured an instant takeover of the mine were quickly neutralized. Their hands shifted back to the reins of their horses.

Ben smiled. 'Seems like you have your answer, Sheriff. Now get off'n my land and take your barking Rottweiler with you. And I would advise you not to come back. Because if'n you do, expect a hot-leaded reception.'

'You're making a big mistake, Cavendish,' said the sheriff, trying to regain his lost reputation as a tough lawdog.

'The law is on Mayor Daley's side. Resisting will only make things worse for you in the end.'

'We'll take our chances,' snapped Cavendish. 'Now git!'

5

A Burning Issue

The posse spurred off back down the canyon, led by Digger Brown. After crossing Catalina Creek they disappeared from view into a clump of cottonwoods. That was where the hardcase called a halt.

'What are you stopping here for, Brown?' the sheriff muttered, forcing some asperity into the query.

'I don't know about you guys,' the Aussie tough retorted, ignoring the weak-kneed lawman, 'but I for one ain't gonna let some hick miners get the better of me.' He tapped his head of curly black hair. 'That Stetson was shipped in by the man himself from El Paso.'

The incident had dented Brown's pride. As a hard-nosed tough guy, he

deemed it a blatant insult and wanted revenge.

'I'm with you there,' Mancos backed up with his hotheaded associate.

'What do you have in mind, Digger?' enquired a bulky dude who went by the name of Pieface Bundy on account of his penchant for pastries. If proof were needed, a bulging torso was the visual evidence. Most jiggers would rail against such a handle. Pieface, on the other hand, welcomed it. He claimed that having a nickname gave him kudos.

Brown was not slow to respond.

'There are six of us,' he expounded firmly. 'I say we ride back and take 'em out. The suckers won't be expecting that if we go in all guns blazing.' He looked around expectantly at the others. 'So what d'yuh say, boys? Are we real men or just a bunch of lily-livered spinsters?'

'I ain't so sure about making a frontal assault,' cautioned a scrawny little jasper called Monk Wickenburg. 'That guy with the rifle knew how to shoot.

You of all people should know that.' Removing his hat he tapped the bald monastic circle on his head meaningfully.

Mancos laughed at that prickly comment. But the wry simper was instantly removed from the Kid's pretty-boy features by a glowering scowl from Brown.

'Yeah!' butted in the sheriff. 'And he said the others were just as good, even the girl. Our job is to report back to Daley. There was no mention of running them out of the canyon.'

'But it looks like that's the only way he's gonna get his hands on that mine,' another posse member insisted.

'What did I tell yuh?' snapped Brown.

'There is another way,' said Pieface. All eyes turned towards the corpulent rider. 'What say we burn 'em out. The Indian can use his bow to loose a couple of fire arrows on to the cabin roof. That should drive the varmints out into the open.'

The attention of the posse swung towards Pawnee Bill, who had thus far remained silent. The half-breed had never known his father, who had been an itinerant trader. After learning that the young Pawnee squaw with whom he had dallied was pregnant, the degenerate had split the breeze faster than a New Mexico roadrunner.

Like all such progeny of mixed race, Bill was scorned by both red and white. It was his skilful use with the bow and arrow that had attracted the attention of the one-eyed Aussie, himself something of a misfit. The two had joined forces and had been running together for the last two years.

'What about it?' asked Brown of his buddy.

Bill's face looked as if it had been carved from a block of red sandstone as he mulled over the suggestion. Then slowly the patrician head nodded in accord. 'No problem for Indian,' he grunted.

Brown smiled. 'Are we agreed then?'

Angling a disdainful glance towards the sheriff, he silently defied the lawman to refuse. Tomlin knew when he was outnumbered. He shrugged, accepting the majority decision. 'Then let's get to it.'

The six men dismounted and crept towards the edge of the tree cover. A distance of one hundred yards separated them from the cabin, across a stretch of open ground that sloped downwards at an increasingly steep angle to the creek.

The log flume meandered down the gradient towards the creek below on one side. Slanting diagonally across the slope was a roughly constructed set of rails coming from the mine.

The posse crouched in the trees on the opposite bank of the shallow waters.

'OK, Bill,' whispered Brown. 'Do your stuff.'

'Need some fire material,' the Indian announced.

None of the others had thought about that.

'Sap from that creosote bush should work,' declared Bundy.

He hurried across to a nearby clump and hacked off the bark, revealing the plant's treacly juices. Untying his necker, the rotund deputy daubed it thickly before handing it to the Indian.

Bill tore up the red cloth and wrapped each piece around the shafts of three arrows. Then Digger Brown applied a lighted vesta to each. The sap hissed and sputtered producing a small flame that quickly spread over the doused cloth.

Allowing the flame to strengthen, Bill then notched the first arrow. He hefted the bow. In a single fluid motion he loosed off without appearing to draw a bead on the target. Before it was halfway to the distant cabin, the other two arrows were likewise dispatched on their lethal journey.

All three missiles struck the tinder-dry roof. Within seconds, smoke could be seen rising from the tarred felt.

Digger Brown clenched his right fist

in triumph. 'Well done, Bill!' he hollered. The Indian brimmed with pride. Without wasting time, Brown rapped out, 'Get ready, boys. It's showtime. Soon as they come out, let the bastards have it.'

Inside the cabin, Ben Cavendish looked up from a plate of refried beans. A slight noise on the roof had caught his attention.

'Must be a varmint or bird,' Shona intimated, doing her best to tackle the unappetizing meal delivered by her father. A few minutes later her nose wrinkled. 'Is that burning wood I can smell?' she said.

Ben sniffed. 'Sure is. Maybe the stove has rekindled itself.' He aimed a searching regard towards the cooking range.

'It isn't the stove, Pa,' exclaimed his daughter. 'Look!' Her finger was pointing at the cabin roof.

Wisps of smoke were dribbling through the slatted beams. Ben lurched to his feet to catch a better look. Then

79

the full horror struck him.

'The cabin's on fire,' he shouted.

'How in thunder did that happen?' asked a bemused Shona Cavendish.

'I don't know but we need to douse it quick afore the whole place goes up in flames.' Without waiting for an answer, Ben grabbed a bucket and hurried outside where a water barrel was always kept filled.

Almost before Shona had posed the query as to the fire's origins, the answer had flashed into her mind. The posse must have decided on the terminal course of action suggested by that one-eyed galoot who was all for a fight. And the critters must be out there now, just waiting for the cabin's occupants to leave.

She cried out in an attempt to stop her father falling into the deadly trap.

But to no avail. Gunfire erupted from the edge of the clearing. A piercing howl of pain informed her that he had been hit. She hurried over to the door and peeped out. There he was, splayed

out on the ground, blood pouring from two injuries in his leg and shoulder.

A groan, however, told her that he was still alive.

All the girl's instincts urged her to dash outside and save him. But that would be pure suicide. She also would be cut down in a hail of bullets. Right on cue, slivers of wood were ripped from the veranda as more shots were fired.

Quickly Shona slammed the door. She grabbed a hold of her rifle and pumped a couple of rounds towards the hidden gunmen. She had little hope of hitting anything, but at least some form of retaliation made her feel better.

A glance up at the ceiling told the girl that the fire had taken a firm hold. It was already crackling and spitting above her head. Now tongues of flame could be seen licking through the blackened slats. Another few minutes and the whole lot would collapse.

She needed to get out, and quick. There was only one other exit from the

cabin. A rear window gave on to a narrow passage that led behind the cabin. It was where the rail tracks emerged from the mine entrance. Randy was working in there now. He must have heard the shooting and cottoned on to what was taking place.

Without further ado the girl hustled into the back room and scrambled through the window. Head bent low, she scurried across to the dark open void of the mine and disappeared inside.

'Where's Pa?' snapped Randy Cavendish, pumping a shell down the slope to where puffs of smoke could be seen.

'He took a couple of bullets trying to get some water to douse the fire.' Tears were welling up in the girl's eyes. 'I tried to stop him but it was too late.'

'Is he . . . ?'

'Not yet,' she answered dispatching her own lead-filled response towards the hidden assailants. 'But he will be unless we can do something.'

Jaw clamped tight shut, Randy had

little to offer. They were trapped in the mine with no way out except down the slope where the five gunmen were waiting. And with no water and only a few rounds of ammunition between them, the future looked decidedly bleak.

Shona sensed her brother's desperation. She had escaped one threatening catastrophe only to find herself in an equally dire situation. There was no point in surrendering. These jaspers had made it perfectly clear that death was their only escape.

The stand-off continued for the rest of the afternoon. But the dice were all loaded in favour of the posse.

At the bottom of the slope Wes Tomlin had decided to inject some starch into his backbone. Digger Brown was trying to take over the posse and make him out to be a spineless milksop. Tomlin could not allow that to continue if he was to remain in the job of sheriff once they returned to Jacinto.

The miner's cabin was a roaring

inferno, Ben Cavendish had been shot down and was likely dead. Daley was going to hit the roof when he learned what had occurred. This take-over was supposed to have been carried out through the due process of the law. Somehow, he had to retrieve the situation. First thing was to offer the trapped miners a way out.

Sucking in his breath, the sheriff gave his orders. 'This is all wrong,' he stated with authority. 'Our job was to give these people the chance to leave here peaceably.'

'You saw how that stubborn old cuss reacted,' Brown shot back. 'These critters want a fight to the death and that's what they're getting.' He let fly another couple of bullets to emphasize his position.

'Well, I'm going to give them the chance to surrender before anyone else is shot down.' Thereupon, the lawman got to his feet and shouted out loud so that the trapped miners could hear him. 'You people ain't going nowhere. If'n

you come out now with your hands high, I'll see to it that no further action is taken against you. And to show this ain't no cheap trick, I'm coming out into the open.'

Inside the mine entrance Randy was thinking hard. The full force of the sun was blazing down into their eyes. His tongue felt like a lump of hard leather in his mouth. Shona looked even worse. Stay where they were to fight it out and they would be buzzard bait before sundown.

'What do you say, sis?' he croaked. 'The guy seems like he means it.'

Tomlin had pushed through the screen of bushes. Yet even before he had time to speak further a single shot erupted from the tree cover. The lawman threw up his arms and fell to the ground.

Then another voice boomed out in a discordant Aussie drawl.

'The sheriff has just resigned from his post,' came the brittle wisecrack. It was accompanied by a mirthless guffaw.

'And I'm assuming command. Ain't that right, boys?' The other members of the posse were too shocked to react other than by grunting their assent. 'The name's Digger Brown. Remember that when you're stoking up the fires of hell.'

The posse settled down to await developments. Time was on their side.

'How we gonna explain Tomlin's death?' asked a nervous Kid Mancos. The others were equally keen not to be blamed for Brown's madcap actions.

He calmed their fears by assuring them that the gunning down of the sheriff would be blamed on the miners and was reason enough for the varmints to be eliminated permanently.

'And Daley will save on having to make that pay-out,' the one-eyed killer highlighted. 'And I'll make darned sure that our actions today will earn us all a hefty bonus.' The distinct possibility of extra cash perked up the rest of the posse. 'How's about you brewing us all a pot of strong coffee, Bill?' he said to

the Indian, 'while Wick here goes and shoots a couple of rabbits. All this shooting has made me hungry as a wintered grizzly.'

Meanwhile, up at the mine, the shooting of Sheriff Tomlin had shocked the trapped victims of the brutal assault.

'It looks like the sheriff was gunned down by his own posse,' observed Randy.

'What happened, do you think?' asked a bewildered Shona.

'My figuring is that the guy with the funny accent started the ambush,' Randy maintained, 'and when Tomlin objected, he was shot down.'

'So it follows that we'll be blamed for the killing.'

'Worse than that, Shona. They won't want any witnesses left alive to reveal the truth of the matter. Unless we get out of here soon, we're going the same way as Pa and the sheriff.'

'What are we going to do?' A note of fearful panic had crept into the girl's

usually relaxed demeanour.

Her brother was struggling with the same implacable predicament. He tried to swallow but his throat was raw. After checking his rifle, he announced that the old Henry carbine only had six bullets left.

'I've only three.' The girl's reply emerged as a guttural croak. Their wild eyes desperately searched for a way out.

That was when Randy's gaze lit upon the mine cart. The rails on which it moved cut obliquely across the slope down to the creek. Rolling downhill under its own momentum the cart normally came to an abrupt halt at the bottom, where it was then emptied and the contents sifted.

Randy surmised that if he could get the thing moving and then climb inside, he would have sufficient cover to launch a surprise retaliation against the gang. Quickly he broached the idea to Shona.

'Are you sure it will work?' Scepticism laced her query.

Randy shrugged. 'Anything is better

than just waiting for the end here. And that can't be far off.'

Crazy to be sure. But what the heck! This was their last chance. Better to go down fighting than skulk up here like rats in a trap.

'Then go for it,' Shona agreed with a renewed sense of do or die in her voice. 'I'll give you my three bullets' worth of covering fire once you get moving.' She smiled. Their hands met in a valedictory display of sibling affection as Randy struggled to manhandle the heavy wooden cart into motion.

Running along beside it, he swung his legs over the side and crouched down. Only his head showed above the side.

Slowly the cart began to lumber forward, steadily gathering momentum as the gradient increased. The rumbling growl of the iron wheels soon attracted the attention of the besiegers. Rocking and swaying like a runaway locomotive, it plunged ever downhill on its frenetic dash. Randy was forced to cling on for

dear life. Gripping the upper edges tightly, he desperately prayed that the cart would not derail.

The diagonal tilt of the railroad from left to right forced the bushwhackers out into the open. That was when Shona opened up.

Momentarily stunned by the sudden act of retaliation, Digger Brown could only stare open-mouthed at the approaching mine cart. But he soon recovered from the shock as one of the girl's few remaining bullets scored a furrow across his exposed head. It was only a flesh wound but it stung the braggart into action.

'Get the bastard!' he yelled, letting fly with his revolver while backing away. More panicky shots rang out in response when the rest of the gang cottoned on to what was happening. But they all went wide.

Randy took full advantage of his surprise fight back. Levering the rifle he pumped all his remaining shells at the men below.

'Yeehaa!' he screamed. Adrenalin pumping through his body had doused any sense of fear. A reckless abandon had permeated his whole being. 'That'll teach you bunch of vipers to tangle with the Cavendish clan.'

His Scottish highland ancestry now took control. The raucous battle cries from a delighted Randy Cavendish filled the dust-laden air as one of the gang threw up his arms. Monk Wickenburg quickly followed. The others backed away under the relentless onslaught, following in the wake of Digger Brown. They had no idea that the attacker was down to his last two bullets. Erratic shooting resulted in bullets whining and ricocheting off the onrushing cart.

But Randy was well concealed. Nearing the bottom of the slope, he leapt out of the hurtling cart where the two dead posse members lay. He grabbed hold of a discarded rifle and hid behind the body of Wickenburg. He stepped up his rate of fire.

A grin of satisfaction broke across his

sweating face as he heard Brown urging his followers to quit the scene before any more of them were gunned down. Randy's bold initiative had worked perfectly. The craven deputies had been completely routed. Pounding hoofs informed the attacker that they had quit the battlefield in total disarray.

6

Mission to Banner

Randy picked himself up, hardly able to credit that he had beaten off the posse. The cart had crashed into the earth mound by the creek and now lay on its side. But the euphoria of moments before was squashed when he looked back up the slope to see Shona bending over their father's prostrate form.

Quickly he scurried back up the open ground to join her.

'How is he?'

'Still breathing, but he's lost a lot of blood,' replied his distraught sister. Like her brother, she counted their recent besting of the gang for nothing if their father didn't pull through. 'We need to get him to a sawbones fast,' she urged.

'The only one within fifty miles is at Jacinto,' muttered Randy.

Brother and sister held each other's apprehensive gaze. They knew in their hearts that there was no other choice.

Randy spoke the words that each was thinking. 'We have to go there and risk another showdown. Try to reach Tucson and Pa will surely die.'

Shona nodded. 'You're right, and the sooner we set off the more chance he has of pulling through.'

With young Brad having commandeered the wagon, their only option was to build an Indian *travois*. Randy immediately set to work.

Two long poles were slung crosswise over the back of the spare horse and tied together resting on the saddle horn. At the rear, a platform was secured and covered with plenty of blankets, upon which Ben Cavendish was carefully laid. The contraption provided a surprisingly comfortable ride.

Randy had learned the art from a friendly tribe of Plains Indians one time while working for the cattle breeder in Kansas. That was where he had met

Laramie Juke. The two had become unlikely allies before parting to go their separate ways over a year before.

It was a morose duo that drew to a halt outside the small town of Jacinto some four hours later. Shona had done the best she could to dress her father's injuries. But the bullet wounds were still leaking blood. More worrying, though, he had still not regained consciousness. The girl was concerned by her father's ragged breathing, which did not bode well.

On the way to Jacinto, they had determined to face up to any charges that were laid against them regarding the killings at Tascosa Canyon. Right was on their side. It was the posse who had precipitated the gun battle. And it was Digger Brown who had bushwhacked the sheriff.

What the skunk had failed to heed was that he had shot the lawman in the back. There was no way that either of the prospectors could have been responsible for that. To prove their case, the

body of the deceased sheriff had been brought along. So they were hopeful that no charges would be brought against them.

Nonetheless, where a varmint like Highspade Jack Daley was concerned, nothing could be taken for granted.

Randy nudged his horse forward with the travois animal following behind. Slowly they edged up the main street. News of the deadly incident had clearly reached the town. By this time, Brown would have spread the story of their alleged attack upon the posse.

Citizens paused to stare at the strange spectacle. Suspicious looks followed their progress up the street. But hardly any of them were sympathetic. Randy's hand rested on his gun butt, just in case anybody decided to take the law into their own hands.

Nobody moved.

Curiosity was the principal mood of the watchers.

Then Maisie Dobson, Shona's friend and the town's only dressmaker, rushed

out of her shop to join them. Randy had been walking out with the young woman since last month's Saturday dance.

'I heard what Daley's bodyguard is spreading around,' the feisty woman blurted out, gripping her beau's hand, 'and I don't believe a word of it. And that goes for a lot of other folks too.'

'We'll tell you all about what really happened once we've got Pa settled,' Shona assured her friend.

Only when the small party reached the far end of the street, where Doc Farthing had his clinic, did the acute tension ease up. Shona hurried inside the surgery, appearing moments later with the elderly medic. Farthing immediately gave instructions for the patient to be carried inside.

Normally a reserved man who gave little away, the doctor was visibly shocked to see the body of the sheriff in the wagon.

'H-how did this h-happen?' he stuttered before regaining his composure.

His eagle eye had immediately spotted that the lawman had been shot in the back.

'He and a posse came to deliver an ultimatum to evict us from our mining claim in Tascosa Canyon,' said Randy making a purposeful attempt to remain calm and unruffled. 'But we sent them away with a few choice words.' Noting the doctor's reproachful frown he hurried on: 'They started the shooting, not us.'

'It appears that some rebellious members of the posse decided to take the law into their own hands.' Shona continued the account after returning from supervising her father's care inside the small hospital. 'They clearly resented our interference. We managed to turn the tables and drove them off. But it was a close-run thing.'

Doc Farthing's face relaxed. He stroked his pointed chin. 'Wes Tomlin wasn't much of a law officer,' he declared, 'but that's no excuse for a back-shooting.' Then he called to a couple of onlookers.

'Have the sheriff's body deposited in the mortuary.'

'I'll have to report this to the town council,' the medic continued. 'They can arrange the funeral and ask the county commission for a replacement law officer. Way things stand in this town, we sure need one.'

The doctor moved away, shaking his head in bewilderment. In somewhat of a daze, the two young people mounted up and swung their horses around. They plodded back up the street and drew to a halt outside the dressmaker's establishment, unaware that they were being observed by a certain party who was riled at the way the situation was developing.

Jack Daley scowled at the couple from the upstairs window of his office.

He had been given an entirely different interpretation of the recent debacle by Digger Brown. According to his bodyguard, the blame for its tragic outcome lay with the Cavendish brood. They had resorted to the gunplay

leading to the sheriff's demise.

Daley stamped around the room. A glowering cast was pasted across the oily features. 'This is the last thing I wanted,' he railed at the Aussie hardcase.

'But I figured that you'd want those wasters removing from the picture, boss,' the desperado whined. 'That's why me and the boys returned fire when they decided to shoot it out.'

'You durned clown!' hollered the irate official.

Brown pursed his lips. His single eye glimmered with wrath. Nobody spoke to him like that. His hand strayed to the gun on his hip. The last critter to insult him had ended up on boot hill. But Daley paid good bucks for his heavy-weight services. So the one-eyed tough swallowed his pride and curbed his fiery temper.

'This was meant to be handled without any violence.' Daley continued with his ranting diatribe unaware of the protector's seething resentment. 'I don't want

folks suspecting the truth as to how I came to take possession of that mine. And make no mistake, I aim to get my hands on it — one way or another. Now you've gone and put paid to that. There's gonna be a heap of explaining to the council if'n I'm to come out of this with a clean sheet. So you better hope I succeed.'

Concluding his vehement harangue, the mayor fell silent.

'So what are we going to do now?' asked Hymie Weiss, who was also peeved that his legal declaration had met with such a lethal result.

Daley had been thinking along similar lines.

'Those turkeys are clearly not going to be shifted by edicts and by-laws,' he asserted, having come to a decision. 'So we have to resort to the same tactics.'

'What do you have in mind, Jack?' asked Weiss. His pudgy features had crinkled with dismay. 'Don't expect me to strap on a gunbelt and join you in a shoot out. That ain't my style.'

'Don't worry, Hymie,' the mayor replied scornfully, 'I wouldn't ask you to dirty those lily-white hands.'

The lawyer's face flushed, but he wasn't given the chance to reply. Brown had seen an opportunity to get back in favour. He shouldered himself off the wall and handed the mayor a copy of the *Arizona Herald*, which he had been casually reading.

'Take a look at this article, boss,' he said, pointing to a commentary sporting a bold headline that read: *Notorious Hired Gunman clears up in Banner.*

The report went on to explain how the infamous bounty hunter, Shotgun Murphy, had single-handedly cleared the town of a gang of Mexican *bandidos* who had been terrorizing the residents. There was a grainy pen drawing of the legendary gunslinger clutching his trademark Greener shotgun.

A smirking face stared out from the picture. Hooded dark eyes appeared to issue a challenge to anybody who

thought to end his run of successful assignments. Shotgun Murphy was not a varmint to be taken lightly.

On this occasion it appeared that Murphy had sided with the law-abiding elements who had hired him. But the menacing hunter was equally at home hiring his services out to anybody willing to pay his fee, from whatever side of the law they hailed.

Having read the article, Digger Brown acknowledged to himself that he was not in the same league as the infamous gunman. Not that he would ever admit that out loud. But maybe they could work together if the guy was open for hire.

Daley read the article twice before handing it to the lawyer.

'This guy sounds just right for flushing out that Cavendish crew,' he averred. 'What do you say, Hymie?'

'We'll need to ensure that our names are not associated with a gun-happy tough like Murphy,' the lawyer contended vigorously. 'If anybody at the

county seat discovers who hired him, we're finished.'

Daley strolled over to the safe in the corner of the room. Twirling the combination lock he swung open the heavy iron door and extracted $500 in greenbacks, which he handed to Brown.

'Head up to Tucson and see if'n this guy is still around,' Daley ordered. 'If not, then find him. There'll be another five hundred on the successful completion of his mission. You can fill him in on the details. Then get back here pronto. Savvy?'

'What if this jasper ain't there?' asked a sceptical Digger Brown. He was a hard-nosed minder, not a detective.

Daley huffed with exasperation. 'Use your imagination. Just find him. You could start by making enquiries at the newspaper office where this article was written.'

'Sure thing, boss,' avowed the bodyguard, trying to inject a measure of enthusiasm into the reply. 'You can count on me.'

That was what Daley wanted to hear. 'Do this job right and there'll be a hefty bonus coming your way,' the mayor declared with a casual smile. Brown's lone eye widened. A baleful glare from his boss, however, soon scotched the minion's delight. 'But get it wrong and there won't be a safe place for you to hide anywhere in the territory.' His meaning about the tough disappearing with the dough was evident.

* * *

Brown set off for Tucson at first light the next morning.

It was an uneventful trip and having arrived at the bustling settlement, he went straight to the offices of the *Arizona Herald*. But the editor was of no help. He had received the story from a passing drifter. The guy had sunk the fee he had been paid in the nearest saloon, then left town the next day.

Brown realized that his only option was to continue north up through

Sedona Canyon to Banner, some four days' ride away.

As soon as he arrived in the town the gunman sought out the largest saloon. It stood in a central plaza, which boasted the tallest flagpole Brown had ever seen. A flag advertising the town's *raison d'être* fluttered in the breeze — a cluster of pine trees. Banner was a logging settlement.

The gunman tied off and wandered across the plaza to the saloon. That was the place to learn whether Shotgun Murphy was still around. A large model of a pink pig sporting a pair of silver wings and a beaming smile was fastened on to the veranda fronting the saloon. As intended, it brought a like response from Digger Brown.

Inside, the Flying Pig was much like a host of other such establishments that satisfied the inner needs of the frontiersman. Most of the customers were loggers. Banner was close to the largest tract of pine forest in the territory. The trees were gradually being cut down to

satisfy the country's voracious appetite for timber.

The newcomer ordered a beer. After a few pleasantries to break the ice, Brown posed the vital question concerning Shotgun Murphy's recent exploits. The bartender was more than happy to oblige. A detailed account of the incident followed.

'What happened to the greasers that he tangled with?'

Piggy Mulligan slung a thumb to his rear. A hearty guffaw rumbled up from his wobbling belly. 'All buried in a single grave in the town's cemetery.'

Brown nodded. He was impressed.

'That's one mean fella,' warned the 'keep, placing a second foaming glass on the counter. Brown sank half the pot in one swallow. 'Get on his wrong side and you'll be heading up the same hill to join 'em.'

'Did he stick around after doing the business?'

Brown sunk the other half of the beer waiting for the loquacious guy to

continue. Bartenders were like that. They couldn't stop talking.

'Only for a couple of days. Spent most of the time in here. He sat right over there,' Piggy Mulligan pointed over to a table in the corner, 'not bothering anyone, when this jasper walks in. The guy stopped in the doorway eyeing up the customers. When his gaze lit upon Murphy, his mouth twisted into an ugly pout. Straight away I could tell there was gonna be trouble.' Piggy was well into his stride. 'So I grabbed for my own sawn-off which I keep under the bar. Problem was, it weren't there. Then I remembered. The trigger had snapped and Maggs Randle, the gunsmith, was repairing it.'

Piggy's face was red and flushed, his round eyes popping like one of his namesake's. Brown was all ears. Impatiently he urged the porcine bartender to resume his story.

'So what happened?'

'I cussed my bad luck. But no way was I about to get involved in a shindig

without that Loomis,' huffed Mulligan. 'Anyway, this fella stamps across and lumbers to a halt in front of Murphy. My heart was in my mouth. 'You shot my brother over in Snowflake,' the guy growled. 'Now I'm gonna even the score.' You could tell from his slurred voice that the poor sap had been drinking to build up his courage. Then he went for his gun.'

Once again the barman paused to draw breath and mop his brow. Recollection of the violent altercation was making him sweat all over.

'He was fast. No doubt about it. But Murphy had that shotgun of his'n all ready and cocked under the table. The guy didn't stand a chance. Twenty-gauge of choked buckshot blew a hole in his chest you could fit a dog inside. Then Murphy just blew the smoke away, cool as you please. Casually resting the gun on his shoulder, he stood up and left without uttering a single word.'

'That's one helluva tale you tell,

bartender.' Brown was now sure that Shotgun Murphy was the right man for the job Daley had in mind. He smiled, pouring a third beer down his throat before adding, 'This jigger sounds like the man I'm after. Any idea as to where he went from here?'

The barman informed him that the hired gunman had left two days earlier but he had no idea of the direction Murphy had taken.

'You want to hire him or kill him?' enquired the curious barman.

Brown merely tapped his nose, slammed the empty beer pot on the counter and departed, leaving the bald Piggy Mulligan scratching his pink dome.

The problem for Digger Brown was that he still had to locate the gunman. Wandering down the street, he set his brain to thinking, not something it was used to doing. The grey matter began to stir somewhat reluctantly. So how was he going to learn where Murphy had gone?

7

Shotgun Murphy

Then something reminiscent of a brainwave occurred. A smile broke across the searcher's swarthy visage. His good eye flashed. One person likely to have knowledge of Shotgun Murphy's next destination was the telegraph operator. The hired gun was more than likely to have taken advantage of the new-fangled invention to communicate with potential employers.

He sauntered into the office and posed the question. Following some brisk negotiations, a wad of greenbacks was exchanged and Brown had secured a copy of the telegram he was seeking.

It read: *Job at Farmington, New Mexico. Bring equipment for elimination of vermin. Top pay offered. Ask for Grant Mitchell.*

A wry smirk broke over Brown's face. No indication that the proposed job was anything other than extermination of rats on a farm, or the like. Doubtless, Murphy had dispatched a similarly veiled reply.

I like your style, Brown muttered to himself.

In truth, he would have preferred to see the guy in person. But Farmington was at least a week's ride. A telegram was much more convenient. Quickly he wrote down his own message on a slip and handed it to the telegraph operator. It was similarly written in disguised terms.

'How long do you figure before I get a reply?' he asked.

'If'n the recipient gets it lickety-split, ain't no reason why it shouldn't be here by tomorrow morning.' The operator knew exactly what sort of messages were being sent and had decided to capitalize on that knowledge. 'Seems to me like twenty bucks ain't nearly enough for what I'm doing here,' he muttered. 'The way I figure it, a round hundred would

certainly keep my mouth shut.'

Brown scowled back at the devious polecat. In a second his gun was palmed and jabbing in the weasel's ear.

'Well, the way I figure it, buster,' he snarled, twisting the steel barrel hard against bone. 'If news about our little agreement were to become known, I could come back here and drill your miserable hide full of lead.'

The Aussie tough's alcohol-fuelled breath wafted over the little guy, making the jarring threat all the more spine-chilling.

'Or, to keep my nose clean, I could just inform the editor of the *Herald* all about your betrayal of confidence. Once that gets out, you can say goodbye to this cushy job, and probably the next year of freedom.' Brown grinned wickedly, then waited a moment before adding, 'Your call, buddy. So what's it gonna be?'

'OK, OK,' squawked the operator like a panicking chicken. 'I'll keep quiet.'

Brown patted the agent's greasy

locks. 'Good decision, mister.'

Then he left to sample the delights on offer to lonely travellers in the town. All on expenses as well. If there was one thing that Highspade Jack Daley had never quibbled over, it was his expenses.

Maybelline Spinks' Hot Whorehouse was a good place to start.

★　★　★

Two weeks had passed since Shotgun Murphy had received the telegram inviting him to eliminate a thorny problem in the town of Jacinto. Elimination of the 'rats' in Farmington had only taken up a day of his time. An easy 200 bucks now rested in his back pocket. The cable from Digger Brown had left him curious: he had never been that far south before.

The fee on offer was another incentive. A grand was far more than he had been offered previously. This had to be from some dude with power and influence.

A swift reply of acceptance had followed with the proviso that the first half of the fee be deposited in a new account at the local bank in Tucson under a fictitious name. That way he could draw on it without some nosy revenue official becoming suspicious. Wendle Murphy, also known as Shotgun, was a name that would instantly raise eyebrows.

So here he was, nearing the Esperango relay station some three days' ride from his destination. It was run by a fat Mexican called Pancho Dominguez and his equally plump wife Maria. The daily stagecoach from Flagstaff to Bisbee had just left when Murphy drew his sorrel to a halt outside the relay station.

Some stations offered accommodation to independent travellers when they were not occupied by passengers using the stagecoach. Murphy had arrived at the right time. With the stage disappearing into the afternoon sunshine, he could be certain of securing a good room with de luxe facilities,

namely a bath and a flock bed. He had been on the trail since sunup and was tuckered out.

Hearing the sound of hoofbeats the station manager hurried outside to greet the newcomer. 'Welcome to Esperango, señor,' gushed the portly Mexican, bowing low. 'If it is a room that you are seeking, then you are in luck,' Dominguez fussed, his round face beaming. 'I have one only left.'

Murphy returned the unctuous smile with one similarly contrived. 'So where are all the other guests?' he asked, feigning innocence.

The jumpy manager blushed, knowing that he had been caught out. He burbled, waving his arms around like a demented windmill while trying to think up some plausible explanation. But nothing came to mind. Thankfully, his discomfiture was saved by another man emerging from the door of the station.

'When's grub being served, Pancho?' enquired a tall rangy jasper with curly

blond hair straggling from beneath a tan high-crowned Texas sombrero. An unlit cheroot was clamped between teeth that were even but stained yellow. Nonchalantly leaning against the wall, he struck a match and applied the glowing flare to the smoke.

The appearance of the stranger had driven the idle chitchat from Murphy's mind. It was the Colt revolver slung low on his hip that interested the hired gunman. An old .36 Navy, but well kept and rechambered for cartridge use. An experienced appraisal instantly placed him on guard. This jasper was no tenderfoot.

'You going to introduce me to your guest, Pancho?' drawled Murphy, squaring his broad shoulders.

The fat Mexican breathed an audible sigh of relief.

'This *hombre* is called Laramie Juke. He is a cowboy looking for work,' babbled Pancho, waving his hands around.

In truth, Laramie had quit the Lazy K after receiving a disturbing letter

from the guy who had helped him in Dodge City the previous year. It appeared that Randy Cavendish and his family were being harassed by claim jumpers. So now it was Laramie's turn to repay a favour.

'And you, *señor*, are . . . ?'

The latest arrival also produced a cigar, reaching across to accept the proffered vesta from Juke. Both men eyed each other closely. Unspoken curiosity rather than rancour passed between them.

'The name is Wendle Murphy,' replied the hired gun in his characteristic burr. Smoke emerged from between puckered lips in a series of perfect rings. Then he added, 'Some folks call me Shotgun.' An arm casually indicated the long-barrelled weapon poking from its saddle boot.

Laramie's craggy features remained impassive as his gaze rested on the infamous killing machine. Pancho, however, was more expressive in his reaction. Beady eyes popped wide, the

flabby mouth hung open. A film of sweat broke out across his pudgy features.

Hardly able to get his words out, the Mexican gibbered, 'P-please señor, Pancho n-no want trouble. Marie and good self are just simple *personas* trying to earn living out here for stage company.'

Murphy raised his arms. 'Who's looking for trouble? Not me. You want trouble, Juke?' There was a hard edge to the query that the other man could not ignore.

'If'n trouble comes a-calling, I'll face it.' Then he also waved the notion aside. 'But, as Pancho says, I'm a traveller just passing through.' A loose smile brought a twinkle to his bright blue eyes that markedly eased the tension. 'And a hungry one, too.' The lazy regard shifted to the hovering Mexican.

Pancho Dominguez could thankfully breathe again. But that final comment had got the message through.

'Ah, *sí, sí,* I go now to organize food.'

Pancho's stomach shook with nervous laughter as he gratefully disappeared.

'I ain't booked that room if'n you're wondering,' Laramie said. 'It's all your'n. I'm bunking down in the hay barn.'

'Much obliged,' Murphy acknowledged with a nod. He didn't enquire into the other man's wherewithal, and Laramie did not offer any enlightenment. It was an accepted proviso in the West that a man's business was his own. Only if an issue became personal were enquiries sought.

Both men finished their smokes in silence before entering the single large room that acted as kitchen, dining room and sleeping quarters for the manager and his wife. A few personal adornments covered the bare walls. Otherwise it lacked any form of comfort. Conditions at the Esperango relay station were spartan indeed.

But at least the food was wholesome and plentiful. Hot chilli-beef stew was served with cornbread and washed

down with strong coffee.

'You want another slice of apple pie, Señor Laramie?' asked the assiduous cook topping up the blond cowpoke's coffee cup. For some reason that he had never been able to figure out women always seemed to favour him.

Before he could reply the other guest butted in. 'You can sure fill my plate up, Maria. Ain't tasted better pie since Thanksgiving in Denver.' The señora hastened to obey. Nobody kept the infamous Shotgun Murphy waiting. 'Don't mind if'n I have the last slice do you, Laramie?'

'Be my guest,' reassured the cowboy. 'I'm plumb busting out my britches.'

After the remnants of the meal had been cleared away, Murphy asked if his fellow guest would fancy a game of something to while away the time.

'Sounds good to me,' Laramie acquiesced, hooking a few single-dollar bills out of his vest pocket. 'This is all I have.' He shrugged half-heartedly. 'But what the heck? Lose and I ain't much

worse off. But then again . . .' He left
the rest unspoken, instead offering a
wry smirk. 'How about craps?' A set of
dice were produced and flicked across
the table.

Murphy agreed, noting the deft
handling.

'Looks like you've played this game
before, fella,' he said reaching into his
saddle-bag for a bottle of Kentucky
bourbon. He poured them both a
generous slug.

Bets were placed and the gunman
went first. He shook the numbered
cubes, all the while watching his
opponent like a hawk.

Not that there was anything but luck
involved in this game. It was a pure
gamble, although that didn't stop
players from professing a skill in the art
of throwing the dice. It was all part of
the tactics employed to unnerve oppo-
nents. There followed a luck-inducing
blow on the closed fist before the dice
were sent skimming across the table
top.

Laramie then made his play, followed by his opponent. So the contest progressed, each player winning some and losing some.

Then, slowly, Juke began to forge ahead.

As Murphy lost more heavily, his betting likewise became more reckless. At the same time, the bottle of hooch quickly disappeared down his throat. A struggle to control his rising temper festered in his soul. But the hired gunslinger had not survived for this long in his precarious line of work without remaining cool and detached under pressure.

All too soon, the inevitable conclusion was reached. Murphy was cleaned out. That was when the final bet was suggested by Juke.

'All this dough,' the cowboy evenly offered his rival, pushing the heap of grubby notes into the centre of the table, 'for your room.' He waited for the meaning to sink in. 'So what d'you say, is it a bet? Win and you take the lot.

Lose and I keep the dough, and take the room.'

Murphy returned the stare. But his expression remained blank and impassive. He concurred with a single brisk nod. For a long second or three the two men faced each other like two pugilists awaiting the signal for the last round.

Then Murphy made the last throw. The dice skidded across the uneven surface, bobbing and jostling like a pair of drunks before coming to a nerve-shredding halt. All eyes focused on to the white dots displayed. The result had not gone his way. A low hiss trickled from between Murphy's gritted teeth.

'If'n I didn't know better,' he murmured, 'I'd say that these dice were loaded.'

Then, without uttering another word, he picked up his gear and went outside.

Both Pancho and his wife had been on tenterhooks while the game had been progressing. The manager was certain that trouble would erupt when the hired killer lost the bet. It therefore

came as a huge relief when Murphy quietly departed.

Man and wife fussed about, waiting for the sparks to fly. But nothing happened. It appeared that the infamous gunnie had accepted his loss with dignity. Nonetheless, Pancho addressed the cowboy in words barely above a whisper.

'That fellow is one *poco firme hombre*, Señor Juke, bad medicine,' Pancho warned casting a wary eye towards the door expecting the hired gunman to come charging in at any moment, his trademark shotgun blasting. All remained silent. 'You watch step. Not know what he going to do next.'

'Don't worry,' replied Juke with a laugh intended to settle the manager's overwrought nerves. 'I'll leave here at first light. Be long gone afore he wakes up. The guy drank a lot more of that hooch than I did. Can't see him rising earlier than mid-morning.'

With that Laramie Juke retired to the

guest bedroom, where he luxuriated in a hot bath before enjoying a sleep in his first proper bed since leaving Flagstaff.

Maria woke him with a mug of coffee just as the false dawn was brightening the eastern sky. All part of the service afforded by the de luxe room, she assured the surprised occupant. There followed a fully cooked breakfast and even some wrapped tortillas for the onward journey.

It occurred to Laramie that Murphy had missed out on a luxurious night's rest that most guests would have vehemently resented surrendering.

On stepping outside the relay station, he immediately noticed the hired gunman's slumbering form under a cottonwood. The drink must have had a stunning effect in the cool air once he had stepped outside the previous night. Moving closer to ensure that the guy was still out for the count, he sensed a movement. Laramie paused, not wishing to waken the guy whose back was to him.

The sun had just broken over the range of hills behind the relay station. Bands of pink and purple scored the azure backdrop as the new day edged into view. Of more interest to the watcher was the glint of light on metal beneath the apparently sleeping form. Laramie frowned before realizing its significance.

Suddenly everything happened at once.

The supine figure spun round on to his stomach, revealing the hidden shotgun. A blast punctured the silence as both barrels exploded. In a split second Laramie saw that the gunman was attempting to pay off the lethal grudge he had kept on a tight leash all through the night.

The instinct for survival immediately clicked in.

He threw himself to one side as the twin charges of choked buckshot howled past his head and obliterated the relay station signboard. His own gun was palmed in an instant. Two

shots rang out in reply. One went wide, but the second hit the bushwhacker in the neck. Murphy gagged. The scatter-gun dropped from nerveless fingers. Blood spouted from a severed artery, the crimson fountain pumping for a few seconds before the pressure eased down to a slow trickle.

Slowly, Laramie rose to his feet and approached the body. With his pistol trained on the still form, he warily toed the corpse over on to its back. Glassy sightless eyes stared up at him.

Shotgun Murphy was dead.

Exhibiting an equal degree of caution, Pancho Dominguez and his wife circled the still corpse. They could hardly credit that this notorious gun-slinger had been vanquished by a humble cowboy. Laramie could barely believe it himself. He stumbled away, his heart pounding in his chest like a rampant herd of buffalo.

Not that this was the first time he had shot someone. There was that drunken miner in Tucumcari who had

accused him of trying to steel his poke. No amount of remonstrations regarding his innocence had satisfied the inebriate. And all because Laramie had bought his own liquor with gold dust.

The guy had called Laramie a yellow coward when he refused to draw. Such an insult in front of a room full of hard-nosed frontiersmen could not go unchallenged. They had met outside on the street, watched by the whole town, all of whom made certain to keep out of the line of fire.

'Go for your gun, claim-jumper,' burbled Coyote Bob Lander, swaying in the evening breeze.

Laramie just stood there.

The prospector uttered a rumbling growl of irritation, then grabbed for the pistol stuck in his belt. Before he could draw and cock the weapon, he was spinning on his heel as a slug took him in the right forearm. He dropped the gun and fell to his knees.

Laramie had deliberately aimed for a non-lethal hit. Once this jasper sobered

up, he would realize how close he had come to shaking hands with the Reaper.

But Shotgun Murphy was his first killing. Or maybe it was his second.

The next incident had involved an altercation over a saloon gal in Cimarron. He hadn't hung around long enough to find out if'n that critter had survived. The only thing Laramie could recall was all hell breaking loose in the Crystal Palace dance hall when the jasper went for his gun. There was smoke and lead everywhere. And through the mist he'd seen Bearcreek Watson lying on his back with two slugs in his chest.

Gunfighters such as Clay Allison and Wild Bill Longley, with whom he had conversed, both claimed that the first killing was always the toughest, thereafter it became easier. Laramie did not share their self-assurance.

The Mexican interrupted his sombre reflections.

'What should we do with the body?' he asked, unable to take his bulging eyes off the bloody heap.

'We need to hide it someplace where it will never be discovered,' replied Laramie.

'How about old well round back?' suggested Maria. 'It now abandoned because run dry. Good place.'

Pancho gave the proposal an eager nod of accord. 'And then we can cover it with stones to prevent any smell.' His pudgy nose wrinkled.

Now that his nausea had abated, Laramie was eyeing up the shotgun. He picked it up and stroked the polished rosewood stock. It sure was a fine-looking piece of hardware. And since he'd lost his rifle in a dice game two days before in Snowflake, a fresh long gun was not to be sniffed at.

After all, this jasper wouldn't be needing it any longer.

8

Shotgun Charade

Three days later the dusty rider arrived at Jacinto. Slowly he pursued a course down the middle of the broad main drag, studying the place with a curious eye.

It was a typical frontier settlement, much like a hundred others he had passed through. The only difference was the proliferation of adobe structures which hugged the main street on the edge of town. The more familiar wooden buildings with false fronts graced either side of the central sector. Their elaborately painted porticos gave the town an air of quiet prosperity.

It was an illusion soon to be shattered.

If nothing else, this melding of styles was a firm indication to any traveller that he was getting close to the border with Mexico.

One building, however, stood out from all the rest.

Built of red sandstone, it was clearly meant to impress. A gaudy signboard informed all and sundry that this was the office of the Jacinto Town Council.

Laramie dismounted at a hitching rail. After untying his saddle-bags and bedroll, he hooked out the shotgun and sauntered across the street, intending to book a room at the Cactus Flower hotel.

Halfway across the broad thorough-fare his attention was caught by a duo of loud-mouthed jaspers. They had just emerged from a saloon and had clearly imbibed a skinful of hard liquor.

Laramie frowned. He was not averse to partaking of the amber nectar himself although, in his view, it was a touch early in the day for hallooing. These two ought to know better anyhow if'n the tin stars pinned to their vests meant anything. Not exactly glowing examples of their profession, he muttered to himself.

The cowboy slowed his pace to give

the drunkards a wide berth. But their invidious attention was fixed on to someone else heading their way. As they nudged each other like naughty schoolkids their crafty smirks hinted that skulduggery was being mooted. The unfortunate citizen was about to become the butt of their errant humour.

Laramie followed their gaze. His own face visibly hardened into a mask of revulsion. For the object of the ignoble starpackers' effrontery was a young woman. Only when she came to pass by the two braggarts was she apprised of their despicable intentions.

'How's about a kiss then, gal?' slurred Kid Mancos, standing in the girl's way.

Ignoring the leering comment, she tried to push past. But the burly form of the Kid's associate blocked her way. 'Too damned high and mighty for the likes of us then?' Jubal Hacket sneered.

'What do you expect from a Cavendish?' added his swaying partner, making a grab for the girl. But he was too slow.

Shona sidestepped, but in so doing

lost her footing. Her basket of groceries tumbled on to the ground. Mancos saw his chance. Clamping a hand on the girl's arm, he attempted to draw her into a lustful embrace. A desperate struggle ensued. Her nose wrinkled in distaste at the rancid odour of stale beer on his breath.

'Let go of me, you smelly rat,' she howled.

'Watch who you're talking to, gal,' snarled Mancos, struggling to have his evil way.

People in the vicinity paused to watch the sordid incident unfold.

But nobody stepped in to help the girl. Shuffling feet and red faces hinted at guilty consciences. Fear of retaliation from those running the town was a compelling motive not to get involved.

The dubious privilege of being made deputy sheriffs had given these lowlife critters power and influence.

The girl continued to writhe like a disturbed sidewinder in the braggart's grasp. Hacket looked on, enjoying the

uneven contest, awaiting his own turn to humiliate the girl. Then she managed to wriggle an arm free.

A hand raked down the Kid's face, sharp nails drawing a line of blood.

'Aaaaagh!' yelped the bully, slapping a hand to the injury.

His partner howled with laughter. 'Got your hands full there, Kid,' he taunted the young thug. 'You'll be needing a man's help to tame this she-cat.'

Laramie had seen enough.

Though for a moment he was nonplussed. Hearing one of the girl's assailants refer to her as a Cavendish had momentarily shocked him into immobility.

He recalled that Randy had mentioned a sister, although he couldn't remember her name. This girl must be her. And a right stunner she was, too. He could readily understand the actions of the two deputies. But their methods of courtship were inept and despicable, especially for jiggers meant to uphold the law.

Suddenly, his inertia lifted. If these craven town mice were not prepared to help a damsel in distress, he sure was.

A critter of Shotgun Murphy's ilk would probably have joined in with the pair of lowlifes. But that was not Laramie Juke's way. He had more respect for the opposite sex. This girl needed help and he was the man to supply it.

It was a stroke of good fortune that the distressing encounter had occurred close to a water-storage tank intended for dousing fires.

The Kid had stumbled away from the gantry in his efforts to subdue the victim of his uninvited attentions. But a guffawing Jubal Hacket stood right beneath the huge tank. Laramie jammed the shotgun into his shoulder and aimed it at the outflow stop valve.

A moment to draw a bead, then he let fly with one of the barrels only. Smoke and a load of buckshot exploded in a cacophony of brutal resonance. The single blast was more than enough to

achieve its purpose.

Before anyone had the chance to determine its source, water came pouring forth from the shattered appliance. In a gushing torrent it plummeted on to the guttersnipe standing immediately below. Hacket was knocked off his feet as the vile-smelling liquid enveloped him. Spluttering and bawling, he thrashed about in confusion, unable to comprehend what had happened.

Not prepared to accord either of the braggarts an even break, Laramie turned his attention to Kid Mancos.

The noise of the gunshot and his partner's caterwauling had momentarily halted the young gunnie's reactions.

But he was no pushover and immediately sensed danger to his right from across the street. In a desperate manoeuvre, he tried to turn the body of the girl into a shield. At the same time his right hand dived for the revolver on his hip. Too much hard liquor, however, had slowed his reactions.

His assailant was ready.

Laramie spotted the lunge and drew his own pistol. A single shot blasted the rising gun from the Kid's hand. A howl of anguish spewed from the Kid's throat as the slug tore a lump from his hand. Bits of the pistol flew off in all directions, shattered by the lethal impact of lead on steel.

Mancos was forced to release his hold on the girl who took this welcome opportunity to slug her attacker on the chin. Months of hard labour in a gold mine had built up a heap of muscle, all of which was put behind that almighty punch. Mancos staggered back under the dramatic impact, his eyes rolling.

As a finale to the whole unsavoury episode, Laramie dispatched the second barrel of the Greener, destroying the high crown of the Kid's Texas sombrero. Only the wide brim was left, encompassing a head of greasy black hair. It looked like a plum pudding stuck on a plate.

The humour of the situation was not lost on the spectators.

One onlooker suddenly burst out laughing. That set off a tidal wave of hilarity.

The unexpected racket had not passed unnoticed in the office of Highspade Jack Daley. Seeing his men being made the butt of ribald humour in public brought him out on to the street in double quick time.

'What in thunder is going on here?' he demanded, strutting across the street like a haughty peacock. The laughter was immediately cut short. Nobody wanted to rile the mayor of Jacinto.

It was Shona Cavendish who readily informed him of the sordid incident. 'You should keep your goons in line, Daley,' she hissed out. 'Can't a woman walk the streets of this town in safety any more? To be assaulted by so-called officers of the law is vile and despicable.'

The girl drew herself up, pert nose sniffing at the odious pair of skulking toughs who were cringing under the verbal assault. Nods of approval and

murmurings rose from the crowd of onlookers.

A glint of animosity flickered across the mayor's face when he recognized the victim of the assault. But he managed to display the look of contempt expected from a man in his position of authority. Not wishing to be seen to condone the actions of his own officers, he joined in with the browbeating.

'You pair of halfwits are a disgrace to your profession,' he snarled, injecting all the venom he could muster into the harangue. He meant every word, but not for the reasons assumed by the crowd. 'Now get out of my sight before I dish out some action of my own. I'll deal with you both later.'

Then he turned to address the onlookers. 'Sorry about this, folks. As mayor of Jacinto, I apologize for this offensive behaviour from men in my employ. Rest assured that they will be punished in a suitable manner.'

As a final attempt to restore order and cool tempers, he guffawed at the

injured gunslinger. 'What in tarnation is that sitting on your head, Kid? It looks like a drowned rat.'

That piece of wit certainly perked the crowd up. And there was one further announcement that was always good for enhancing public relations. 'OK folks, the show's over. But to demonstrate that Jack Daley is a fair-minded man, I invite you all to head over to the Elk Horn now and have a drink on me.'

A roar of approval greeted that offer. Daley then raised his arms, ushering the crowd away, but they were already surging towards the open doors of the saloon.

Hoping to escape unnoticed, the two objects of the derision tried to skulk away. But Laramie spoke up before they had the chance.

'Before you pair of varmints crawl back into your hole, pick up Miss Cavendish's groceries and apologize to her for being such bad boys.'

Daley scowled. But at a brisk nod from him the two drunks muttered an

apology, then set about their task. Then they quickly hurried off to lick their wounds, vowing that Shotgun Murphy would pay dearly for shaming them in front of the whole town.

Within minutes, only the girl and her Good Samaritan were left with Mayor Daley.

'I am sorry about that, miss — '

But Shona didn't afford the two-faced trickster the chance to wriggle out of any blame for the incident.

'Don't give me all that eyewash, Jack Daley,' she snapped back. 'I know what your game is. And it won't work. Me and my kin are going to work our claim no matter what you and your lawyer friends try to pull. Send any more of your hired thugs to drive us out and we'll be ready. If it hadn't been for this kind gentleman, I hate to think how this would have turned out.'

'You've got me all wrong, miss,' Daley countered with his most cajoling smile. 'That shoot-out was certainly not my doing.'

Shona ignored the denial, instead offering her saviour a graceful bow.

'Thank you for your help, good sir.'

Hearing the girl call the mayor by name, Laramie was taken aback for a second time. Could this be the cardsharp who had fleeced him back in Dodge City? It had to be. Two guys sporting that handle was a coincidence too far. For the moment, however, he would keep this unexpected revelation safely under wraps. Time was needed to figure out a plan of retribution.

So he responded to the girl's gratitude with his most engaging smile, acknowledging the heartfelt compliment with a flourish by doffing his hat.

'Glad that I was around to help out a lady in distress,' he said.

Beneath an outward layer of respectability Jack Daley was seething. This she-devil was undermining his authority, making him look small to some drifter off the trail. Then he saw the elaborately carved Greener shotgun. The penny dropped.

This guy must be the man he was expecting: *Shotgun Murphy!*

Daley immediately butted in on the mutual display of admiration.

'Seems like you arrived in Jacinto just in time to save this lady's honour,' he gushed, holding out a hand. Laramie took it somewhat reluctantly.

Then Daley emphasized his own grand gesture by proclaiming to the girl, 'Meet the famous troubleshooter, Shotgun Murphy.' Turning his attention back to the newcomer he said, 'Step up to my office for some refreshment, Shotgun. The town would like to offer you a fitting reward for helping this lady out.'

Daley had no wish for anybody to discover that he had sent for the hired gunman. That knowledge had to remain a secret.

As soon as Shona heard that her benefactor was none other than the notorious killer, her attitude manifestly changed. Who in the West had not heard about the devious kinds of

trouble that Shotgun Murphy special-
ized in solving? All of them invariably
ended with that famous long gun being
wielded without compromise.

A dark cloud erased the radiant smile
of moments before. Her suspicions
were immediately aroused regarding the
killer's sudden appearance in Jacinto.
She had little doubt as to what the
reward suggested by Daley would
involve.

Arrowing a reptilian look of abhorrence at the supposed killer, a hiss of
loathing issued from between her
clenched teeth. 'Of all the people who
could have come to my aid, it had to be
Shotgun Murphy. What a letdown!' She
shook her head in mocking derision.
'I'm sure that you and this scumbag
will have a good laugh at my expense
when he hands out that reward.'

Then without another word Shona
swung abruptly on her heel and
stamped across to her horse. She
wanted nothing more to do with the
man. Nevertheless, she couldn't hold

back the tears welling in her eyes. Her handsome paladin was none other than a hired killer. It was deeply humiliating. Keeping her back to the two men, she mounted up and turned to leave.

Laramie hurried over to block the girl's way. The last thing he wanted was to end their brief introduction in such an ignominious fashion.

'You've gotten this all wrong, Miss Cavendish,' he insisted with vigour, trying to grab her reins. 'I ain't the guy you think I am — '

'Get out of the way, Murphy,' shouted the girl, vehemently interrupting before Laramie had a chance to reveal the truth. 'Next time we meet, you'll be facing a lot more than just angry words.'

With that she brushed him aside and spurred off down the street.

'Don't you be worrying about her, Shotgun,' warbled an upbeat Jack Daley taking the supposed gunman by the arm. 'She and her kin are all hot air.' Then, lowering his voice to a murmur

he added, 'I've got the rest of your fee tucked away in the safe upstairs. It's all yourn when the job of ridding Tascosa Canyon of those pesky claim jumpers is complete. It ought to be a cinch for a professional guy like you.'

In the office, they were joined by the new sheriff of Jacinto and Hymie Weiss. Daley made the introductions, pouring them all a generous measure of French brandy.

The lawyer was all handshakes and gushing obsequiousness.

Digger Brown, however, cast a jaundiced single eye over the new arrival. He had been expecting a much more dandified operator. Rumours had come down the grapevine that Shotgun Murphy always wore black leather. If it wasn't for the distinctive firearm he toted, this guy could easily be mistaken for a humble cowpoke. Maybe that was the way he liked to appear, so as to catch his victims on the hop.

Brown was also fuming over the way his men had been made to look like

tenderfoot greenhorns. All to save that Cavendish dame from getting her just deserts. That kind of attitude didn't fit the tough-guy image of a supposed hard ass like Murphy.

There was something not quite right about this guy. He would need watching.

The mayor and his legal associate had taken the newcomer at face value. So, for the time being, Digger Brown would have to accept the hired killer for what he seemed to be.

Assurances were given to Murphy that both sides of the law would turn a blind eye to any chicanery that the hired gunman had in mind in order to complete his mission. Daley filled in his new employee concerning the one-eyed sheriff's recent altercation with the Cavendish outfit.

Brown scowled. He had no wish to have his failure in Tascosa Canyon raked over in front of the famous bounty hunter.

But Daley wasn't concerned with his

lackey's feelings.

'Just so long as my name is kept out of the picture,' he warned the new man, 'you have a free hand. Ain't that so, Hymie?'

'We would prefer that any . . . erm' — the bent lawyer paused to find the right word — 'terminations are made to look accidental. Mayor Daley is running for high territorial office and we cannot afford to have any scandal tainting his good name.'

Brown nodded in agreement. He had high hopes of stepping into the mayor's shoes following Daley's successful election to the county seat.

'And as an added bonus, you are welcome to enjoy the freedom of Jacinto,' the mayor declared with easy magnanimity. 'That means you can have anything you want completely free of charge. Be it a meal, the best room in town or even a dalliance with one of Madame Syn's more imaginative girls.'

Sniggers all round followed this submission.

Laramie viewed these duplicitous toads with thinly disguised contempt. But knowing he had the advantage in the bizarre charade, he was more than willing to enjoy the benefits on offer. Perhaps he would start by cladding himself in some fresh clean duds.

'I'll stick around for a day or two and get the lie of the land,' Laramie indicated, hooking out a cigar from the Mayoral humidor. 'Then I might ride out to the canyon and see if'n these miners can be made to see sense without any force being exerted.'

'Good idea, Shotgun,' agreed Weiss, who was always wary of violent confrontations. 'Much better to settle this matter by negotiation if possible.'

'Mind if'n I join you?' Brown asked rather tentatively.

That was the last thing Laramie wanted: some pawn of Daley's tagging along.

But he purposely delayed the put-off by supposedly considering the request with sound reasoning. 'Perhaps on this

151

first occasion, it would be better for me to go alone,' he said. 'You're known out there so it would be like rubbing salt in the wound. No sense in getting them all riled up. I've perfected my own way of dealing with problems of this sort.' He gave the sheriff a patronizing look of regret. 'That all right with you?'

Brown snorted. He had little choice in the matter. However, he still clung to the hope of joining the famous gunslinger when he made his move. After all, there was still some unfinished business to avenge.

Soon after, the meeting broke up. Laramie promised to let the mayor know when he was ready to ride out to Tascosa Canyon. In the meantime he fully intended to take advantage of the perks on offer.

After kitting himself out with a new suit he moseyed on down to the barber shop. Next stop was the classiest restaurant in town. It was frequented by the wealthier citizens of Jacinto and the food was like nothing Laramie Juke,

cowhand, had ever tasted before.

And all this was free of charge.

Laramie was definitely enjoying the materially plus side of being a notorious gunslinger, not to mention the bowing and scraping that accompanied it. All drinks in the saloons were on the house as well. He was even presented with a new revolver to replace the old Navy Colt when he called into the gunsmith's for some fresh ammunition.

The humble cowhand was rapidly coming to appreciate why men such as Shotgun Murphy relished their way of life. People took notice, listened to what you had to say. Living in the assumed role of the notorious gunman could become a habit difficult to abandon. Sure it was a dangerous life living by the gun. There would always be some jasper wanting to take out the famous gunslinger.

Nevertheless . . .

Then his thoughts drifted back to the girl and how her family were struggling to beat off the craven intentions of

scum like Jack Daley. Shotgun Murphy was a part of that ruthless endeavour.

For a moment the bogus gunman had been blinded to the disparity between right and wrong. It was all a charade, forced on to the good citizens of Jacinto by that lowlife tinhorn, just like his own affectation of the hired killer.

Quickly Laramie shook off the rose-tinted view that had deceived him. There was work to be done and it clearly did not include lining the pockets of crooked deadbeats.

9

Mistaken Identity

There was one more problem that needed sorting out before he could leave town on the next stage of his mission.

His horse had caught a scattering of shot during the fracas at the Esperango trading post. Pancho Dominguez, the manager, was well-versed in the treatment of equine injuries, and some strong horse liniment had temporarily cured the problem. But the animal was still suffering. A visit to the livery man who also acted as the local horse doctor brought bad tidings.

The animal was fit only for the knacker's yard.

'No problem there, Shotgun,' declared Saddleback Sutter, who was as eager to please as all the rest of the business folk. 'You can have the best mount in my

stable.' He led the notorious gunslinger over to a black stallion. 'Jet here will outrun anything on four legs in the territory.'

The guy clearly regretted having to surrender the handsome piece of horse-flesh. And Laramie felt a pang of guilt about taking him. But he needed a reliable mount.

'Don't worry, mister,' he assured the dealer. 'I'll make certain to look after him. And when my business round here is finished, you can have him back.'

Sutter's face beamed with surprise. 'You really mean that?'

The new handler nodded as he levered himself into the saddle. 'Sure do,' he breezed, matching the livery man's grin with one of his own. 'Don't let anybody tell you that Shotgun Murphy never keeps his word.'

With that parting guarantee the hired gunman spurred off, leaving a bemused Saddleback Sutter scratching his head. Hard-boiled killers were not meant to show consideration for their fellow

human beings. This guy didn't quite fit the mould.

Sutter had given him directions for Tascosa Canyon, which was some ten miles to the south-east in the Dragoon Mountains. On two occasions he concealed himself behind some rocks to study his backtrail.

That sheriff had given him some suspicious looks. A cynical jasper, like all lawmen, Brown was quite likely to have followed him. But there was no hint of movement to indicate that he had a tail.

Laramie hesitated over concealing himself for a third time before casting a backward glance. This time he saw it: a swirling wisp of yellow dust a quarter-mile to his rear. Quickly he pulled off the trail into a copse of desiccated juniper bushes. Only just in time. The rider cantered past his place of concealment only minutes later.

Laramie had his lariat spinning in the air. A skilled practitioner in the art of roping on the Lazy K ranch, for him it

was a simple task to ensnare the shifty lawdog. A quick flick of the wrist and Digger Brown was hooked out of the saddle. He landed on the ground with a hard thud.

His hat flew off. Then Laramie received the shock of his life.

Blonde tresses were released instead of the dark greasy hair he'd expected. He had caught himself a girl.

Luckily it was only her pride that was hurt. Shona Cavendish was one tough cookie. But she was angrier than a wild mustang.

Laramie hurried across and helped her up. A stream of unladylike abuse assailed his ears. He was accorded no chance to explain the error beneath the withering tirade. Only his most seductive charm eventually calmed the girl down.

Even so, she was reluctant to forgive him.

'I did save you from those deadbeats in Jacinto,' he purred, urging her to forgive him for the blunder. He was pleased to see that his big blue eyes and

that beguiling half-smile were having a positive effect. 'That must count for something. And how was a guy expected to recognize you in those duds?'

Shona dusted down her trail gear. Her best hat and dress were neatly folded in a bag hanging from the saddle horn. Yet even in such worn clothes, Laramie couldn't help but stare agog at this vision of beauty.

'I stayed over with my friend Maisie Dobson, who runs the dress shop.' Shona was too busy tidying herself to notice the unabashed gawp. 'She's been having trouble with that skunk you're in league with.'

'Listen up, will you?' Laramie snapped, cutting off the girl's biting retort. He immediately regretted the outburst. A contrite apology followed, together with another exhortation for her to hear him out. 'Like I tried to tell you the other day, I ain't Shotgun Murphy. My name is Laramie Juke and I'm a simple cowboy. I was mistaken for Murphy because of that shotgun.'

'So how did you acquire that?' asked the less than convinced vision.

'It's a long story. But you have to believe what I'm telling you,' he implored the girl. 'I was riding out to your place with the intention of working out how we can tackle Jack Daley and his bunch of crooks together. I have my own reasons for wanting to get even with that varmint. It has to do with your brother helping me out of a fix in Dodge City.'

After listening intently to this impassioned plea of innocence, Shona's frosty manner slowly faded on the desert wind. 'I recall now,' she nodded shrewdly, 'Randy mentioned that he'd met some guy up that way before he joined us at the *El Dorado*.'

'Well, he wrote me a letter saying how he needed help with some villains who were after forcing your family off'n the Tascosa claim. So that's why I'm here.'

However, Shona was still torn between two opposing urges. She desperately wanted to believe the mesmeric stranger. What

sort of hardened gunman would behave as he had done in Jacinto? It didn't add up. But her innate caution forbade a rash decision.

Seeing the doubt in her eyes, Laramie pulled out the letter sent to him by her brother. 'Read this if'n you still have doubts,' he urged, handing over the missive.

After reading the content, Shona's tense features relaxed.

'I'm sorry to have doubted you,' she murmured lowering her eyes. 'It's just that . . . well . . . ' Then the floodgates opened. She could not contain the tears. 'All that's happened, with Pa getting shot, and Daley trying to force us out . . . '

Instinctively, Laramie took the girl in his strong arms.

The sudden proximity choked off her mournful wail. She was taken aback by the sudden move. But there was no hesitation on Shona's part in allowing this tall handsome stranger to engage in such intimacy. It felt right. He held her

tightly, allowing the girl's abject sorrow to dissipate in its own good time.

A new aura of closeness had been forged.

Shona readily embraced the warm strength of this man whom she barely knew, yet to whom she felt such a close affinity. It was a feeling she had never previously experienced. A chilled ripple of excitement trickled down her spine. For what seemed like half a lifetime they clung to each other before, somewhat reluctantly, parting.

Much as they both abhorred it, the real world still hovered menacingly over their heads. Before a new dawning could be planned, the unsavoury matter of Jack Daley had to be settled.

'I have a job to do at the far end of the canyon,' she declared with a radiant smile. Her voice trembled, nerves tingling with this novel sensation coursing through her vibrant body. Was this love? She hurried on, not wanting to think about it any longer in view of the injustice still to be overcome. 'The

dam we built to control the waters at the head of Catalina Creek often gets blocked up with debris.'

'Maybe we could clear it together?' Laramie's offer was made so that he might spend some extra time in this lovely creature's company. He felt exactly the same melding as the girl and did not want it to end.

Much as she would have welcomed her new paramour's company, she needed time to think. Time to mull over all that had happened in so short a period. Her emotions were in a frazzled tangle and needed unravelling.

'Best if'n you head direct for the cabin,' she said, trying not to give the impression of a put-down. 'You can introduce yourself to my brother Bradley and acquaint him with what's happened.' Quickly realizing her error, she backtracked, 'Not between us, of course. You know — '

'I'll try and work out a plan of action with him,' Laramie interjected, to save the girl further embarrassment.

A slightly awkward moment followed as they made to part company. It was effectively eased by a cheeky smile from Laramie as he tipped his hat and rode away towards the narrow entrance to the canyon.

He approached the ravine with much on his mind. There was this new found experience of closeness with Shona Cavendish. But equally important was the trouble that she and her kin had blundered into. During the ride he had considered various ideas as to how he was going to play this out. Nothing had come to mind as he emerged from the constricting fissure into the broad amphitheatre beyond.

Still chewing over his change of fortunes with Shona Cavendish, Laramie's thoughts had drifted away from the problem still to be tackled. He was, therefore, caught off guard by a sudden challenge from a rocky ledge to his left.

'OK, mister,' snapped a harsh voice, 'Hold it right there.'

Laramie reined his mount to a halt.

'And keep your mitts away from those guns, else you'll get a taste of Colt lead.' A scrambling of boots on rock followed as the sentinel dropped down behind the rider. 'Now step down off'n that horse slow and easy. And no false moves.'

Brad Cavendish lifted the custom-made Greener shotgun from its scabbard. The young miner cast an admiring look over the fine weapon.

'If I ain't mistaken, there's only one jasper who carries a piece of kit like this,' smirked the young hothead. 'Well, well! So Daley has gone and hired himself the famous troubleshooter, Shotgun Murphy. And I've caught him easy as pie.' Brad coughed out a mocking snigger. 'Don't say much for your talents, now does it, Mr Murphy?'

'You've made a mistake, kid,' replied Laramie. 'I'm not Shotgun Murphy. Daley made the same mistake when I helped your sister out in Jacinto. I was riding out here to see how I could help you defeat him.'

'Humph!' The contemptuous snort was punched out with venom. 'Expect me to believe that load of eyewash? You sneaked out here hoping to get the drop on us and collect a hefty fee for eliminating the Cavendish clan. Well, it ain't worked. Your miserable scheme has been wrecked by none other than Bradley Cavendish.'

The boy uttered a hollow laugh. It was followed by an angry snarl: his hackles were well and truly up.

Without warning, he lunged at the interloper and slugged him over the head with the barrel of his revolver. Laramie was given no chance to avoid the assault. He staggered back and fell to the ground, laid out cold. A trickle of blood soaked through his hair as the angry assailant stood over the still form, breathing heavily.

So irate was the young hothead that he almost hauled off and shot the unconscious man in cold blood. It was the notion that he had caught a famous gunman all by himself that stayed his

trigger finger. This guy had been sent by Daley and he would have vital information to reveal about the bastard's plans.

10

Revelations

It was another hour before Shona returned to the cabin. Hustling cheerily through the door she expected to find her brother discussing the problem involving the gold claim amicably with Laramie Juke. The shock at seeing her knight-errant tethered to a chair with blood dripping down his face was written all over her ashen face.

And there was Brad, gun in his hand, taunting the barely conscious man.

'See who I've caught skulking around outside?' he crowed waving the pistol in a menacing gesture. 'None other than the infamous Shotgun Murphy.'

For a moment, Shona was too stunned to reply.

'But you've got it all wrong, Brad,' cried the distraught girl, rushing across

to the injured man. 'This isn't Murphy.'

'Then what's he doing with that killer's gun?' retorted her brother sceptically. 'More to the point, what's the rat doing in Tascosa Canyon if'n it ain't to spy on us?'

'It's all been a big misunderstanding,' stressed Shona, untying the ropes binding the captive. 'Now help me get him into Pa's room. This wound needs treating.'

'How can you be so sure that he ain't Murphy?' countered Brad, unwilling to believe that he'd made a mistake.

'I just know,' the girl snapped back irritably. 'Just help me with him. And when he is fully recovered, we can learn the whole story.'

Brad Cavendish reluctantly complied, still not convinced that he had slugged the wrong man.

Later, when they had settled the injured man in bed, Shona recalled an article she had read in a newspaper that Randy had brought back from Kansas some time before. It concerned the

exploits of the notorious hired gunman. She quickly hunted it out.

'There!' she announced, jabbing a finger at a photograph. 'This jigger looks nothing like Laramie Juke.'

The photograph had been taken with one of the new picture machines that had recently been invented. It was grainy, but nevertheless the difference was clear enough to satisfy Brad that he had made a mistake. Shona sympathized with her brother's anguish at having attacked the wrong man. She poured him a cup of coffee laced with a measure of whiskey.

'It wasn't your fault, brother. I should have remembered that you'd be keeping a watch for any suspicious characters while Randy is in Tucson.' Their elder brother had gone to the county seat to check with the assay agent about the dubious claim made by Daley regarding his supposed rights to their gold. 'Let's hope that he gets back soon. If Laramie fails to return to Jacinto, things could turn nasty.'

Towards evening the patient awoke with a splitting headache. It was, however, considerably eased by the gentle ministrations of an angel in a plaid shirt.

Laramie emitted a contented sigh. 'I wouldn't mind getting knocked on the head more often if'n this is the result,' he murmured through a bleary haze.

The man who had caused the large swelling above his left ear fussed around like a mother hen, trying to atone for his foul-up.

'Gee, I'm sorry to have slugged you like that, Mr Juke.' The apology was heartfelt. 'It was the gun that done it.' Brad Cavendish screwed up his youthful features in a bewildered twist. 'How come you're toting Shotgun Murphy's trademark hardware?'

'Now that's a story that might take some time in the telling,' Laramie croaked in a subdued tone. He was still feeling rather groggy. 'I'll fill you in when I feel better.'

'Sure thing, I ain't pressing you,'

Brad assured the patient. 'Anything you need, just ask.'

'Got everything I need right here.' Laramie's eyes twinkled as he squeezed Shona's hand. The girl blushed, hurriedly shooing her brother out of the room. 'Go make our guest a fresh pot of coffee.'

'Now that would sure perk me up no end.' Laramie offered the young man a friendly wink to show he harboured no hard feelings.

Later that evening, the steady thud of hoofs could be heard coming up the open ground outside the cabin.

'That should be Randy now,' Brad declared, stuffing one of Shona's biscuits down his throat. 'Let's hope that he has good news.' Nevertheless, the youngest Cavendish hustled over to a window, his rifle at the ready.

'And this time take a good look see before you confront him,' chided Shona.

The mischievous grin on her face was matched by that on Laramie's who

deliberately screwed up his face while rubbing the bump on his head. The action elicited a pained grimace that was the real thing.

A moment later, Brad announced the all-clear as the rider drew to a halt outside. After entering the room Randy shook the dust from his body. The first thing he noticed was the large bandage swathing Laramie's head.

'What in thunder has happened to you, old buddy?' he enquired. Randy had been expecting his associate's arrival for some days, but he had not informed the others that he had written off for his help. 'We met in Dodge City last year,' he confirmed. 'Laramie's come to help us out at my invitation.'

'He told me all about the letter you sent him,' Shona assured her brother. 'We'll give you the lowdown on his erm' — she hesitated not wishing to get her younger brother into any more hot water — 'accident, when you've given us your news. Is that claim of Daley's genuine?'

'Pour me out a cup of coffee first,' croaked Randy. 'My throat is drier than a temperance hall.'

Three cups later the downcast look on their elder brother's face told its own story.

'It's the real McCoy all right,' sighed Randy gloomily. 'The only stipulation is that the claimant must have owned the land in question for at least a year prior to applying for the entitlement. So it looks like we're on a bum ticket here. We can put up a fight. But right, it would appear, is on the side of Jack Daley. Sooner or later, the forces of law and order are bound to win.'

'You've sure changed your tune,' rapped Brad, throwing his brother a look of derision. 'Weren't you the one who was all for holding on here come what may? And now you're prepared to throw in the towel. If'n Pa was here, he'd back me up.'

Randy hung his head, unable to look his brother in the eye. It was true. Ever since he had learned that Daley held all

the aces, a mood of abject depression had enveloped his whole being.

Now it was time for a contemplative Laramie Juke to have his say.

'Talk like that sure ain't from the Randy Cavendish that came to my rescue in Dodge.' Laramie had learned about the whole sorry episode from Shona. 'That guy wouldn't have knuckled under to a bunch of chisellers. I packed in my job on the Lazy K to come out and help you guys. Bow down to tinhorns like that and they will take it as an excuse to ride roughshod over anyone else that gets in their way.'

Brad voiced his vigorous agreement. 'Well, I for one would rather die than give in to Jack Daley.'

But Randy was not to be swayed.

'And you'll get your wish, little brother, if'n we make a stand,' the morose man hit back. 'It's hard to accept, I know. But we haven't been given any choice. It's either cut our losses now and start up someplace else, or fight the full power of the law and end up dead or in jail.'

'Now that's where you're wrong.' They all turned to stare at Shona who had been mulling over the implications of Randy's unwelcome disclosure. 'When I was in town visiting Maisie, we got to talking about the problem of Jack Daley. He's upset a lot of folks, but they're all too scared to do anything about it. He has the law on his side. And any underhand skulduggery is impossible to prove.'

'We know all about that, sis,' Brad interposed. 'What has buying material for a new dress got to do with any of this?'

'If'n you'll give me chance to speak, I'll tell you.' A flinty gaze effectively stilled her young brother's outburst. 'She remembers when Daley arrived in Jacinto. He came direct from Cimarron.' She drew breath before announcing her significant revelation. 'And that was only six months ago. He didn't tell anybody about the land he'd bought over the far side of the canyon. But Maisie's pa is a land dealer in Tucson. And he administered the purchase.'

'In other words, the skunk is trying to cheat us,' enthused a suddenly animated Randy Cavendish. 'He hasn't any legal claim against us at all? Is that what you're saying?'

'Not a scrap!' concurred his sister.

'Then what we waiting for?' exclaimed Brad, drawing his gun and checking the load. 'Let's ride.'

'Hold on there, Brad,' cautioned Laramie. 'If'n we take these guys on with a straight fight they'll win for sure. It will be best if'n I ride back to Jacinto and spin Daley a tale. I could say that I aim to blast you out with dynamite and block up the mine entrance for ever. That should satisfy him. That will give us some breathing space to figure out how to put paid to his game once and for all.'

'Laramie is right,' chipped in Shona. 'No sense in starting a war until we are sure of winning.' Then she cast an anxious eye towards her new love. 'Are you in a fit state to head back there yet?'

'Right as I'll ever be,' said Laramie. 'All I need is a good night's sleep and some of your home cooking. Then I can tackle anything that's thrown my way.'

11

The Devil's Elbow

As Laramie rode down Jacinto's main street he received a startling jolt that brought him to a sudden halt. There, lurching out of the saloon, was none other than Pancho Dominguez. This must be his monthly visit for supplies. The Esperango manager was clearly the worse for too much liquor.

However, a far more important issue was at stake as far as Laramie Juke was concerned. Had the Mexican's over-active mouth run riot concerning his run-in with the real Shotgun Murphy?

He swung his mount over to block the Mexican's unsteady walk towards his wagon.

'Howdie there, Pancho. Remember me?'

Bleary eyes peered back at the

speaker. Then Pancho's face lit up.

'Señor,' he blurted out, making no attempt to conceal his pleasure at the meeting. 'I remember it well. You did the world a great favour by — '

Laramie butted in quickly to prevent the garrulous jigger from divulging his secret. He had to know whether Pancho had indeed mouthed off about the incident. After all, it wasn't every day that one of your guests shoots down a notorious bounty hunter, then assists you to hide the body down a well. Knowing Pancho, he would enjoy the attention such a story created, not to mention the free drinks.

Pancho was swaying, his eyes barely focusing. His blubbery mouth flapped in confusion, but nothing emerged.

'Listen up, you tub of lard,' snapped Laramie impatiently, shaking the rotund greaser's arm. 'Did you say anything in there about Murphy getting shot, and me being the killer?'

The Mexican tried to pull away. Now he had finally discovered his voice.

'Let go of me!' he howled indignantly. 'Pancho say nothing about what happen at trading post. Lips sealed like glue.' He swiped a hand across his now tight-lipped maw.

He wriggled free and dashed across to his wagon, displaying an exceptional agility for one of his bulk. Laramie let him go. He could only surmise that the dude's sudden departure had been precipitated by his own heavy handedness. Or . . .

Could it be a guilty conscience?

It was too late now to learn the truth. Pancho had already whipped up his team and was halfway down the main street, scattering pedestrians in his wake.

The relay station manager's agitated departure had not passed unnoticed by interested parties watching from the front window of the mayor's office.

'Looks like that fat greaser was right when his mouth ran riot,' observed Digger Brown. Daley made no comment. His own mouth was set in a hard

thin line. 'Do you want me to go down and arrest him for bumping off the real Shotgun Murphy?' Brown added.

The mayor shook his head. 'Bring this guy to trial and all manner of shady dealings could come bursting out of the woodwork. Stuff that would shaft my chances of becoming county commissioner if it was made public.'

The devious mind of the official was working overtime as he paced the room in deep thought. A grim expression pushed his black eyebrows together into a single line of menace. After a long minute he came to a halt. A malevolent gaze seared the others in the room.

'This is what we are going to do.'

*　*　*

'Boss want to see you.'

It was a blunt order from the resonant voice of Pawnee Bill. The Indian pushed a thumb towards the council office on the far side of the town plaza.

Laramie was enjoying a much-needed

beer in the Sundowner saloon. He responded with a brisk nod but made no move to comply. Daley could wait. A jasper like Shotgun Murphy would not be rushed.

He gave a nonchalant shrug and slowly finished his beer before deigning to leave the saloon. In the nick of time he remembered to adjust his hat to conceal the bandage swathing his head. He had enough tricky issues at stake without adding to the list.

The 'breed followed close behind.

A knock on the door of the upstairs room was followed by a muted response to enter. Jack Daley was all smiles.

Displaying an affable disposition, he handed the newcomer a cigar. 'Glad you're back, Shotgun,' he said applying a match to the smoke. 'We were getting a mite concerned when you failed to return.'

The use of his pseudonym relaxed Laramie. So Pancho had been telling the truth after all. Tense muscles eased off as he puffed on the cigar appreciating its fine quality. 'I needed more time

to scout the lie of the land and figure out how best to tackle the problem.'

'And did you?' came the brusque question from Digger Brown.

'Dynamite?' The single word was punched out. It provoked a number of raised eyebrows on the faces of those ranged around the room.

'Mind explaining in a bit more detail?' hissed Daley, struggling to maintain the thin smile and conceal a raging anger that now festered within him.

Laramie outlined the bogus plan he had concocted during his trip back to Jacinto. It appeared to satisfy Daley, who suggested that the hired gunman should leave at sunup the following morning. 'The sooner you eliminate these turkeys the better,' he averred. 'Then we can all begin to earn ourselves some real dough.'

He turned to address one of his underlings. Janus Crump was a surly gunman who knew Brown from when they had both operated a claim-jumping scam in Prescott. Brown had sent for him to replace one of the men who had been

killed following the unsavoury episode in Tascosa Canyon.

'You sort out what Shotgun needs from the general store.'

'Sure thing, boss,' replied the hench-man, making for the door and indicating that the bogus gunslinger should follow.

Outside wary eyes watched as a reddish sun sank into an underworld that the ancients believed to contain only death and eternal night. Laramie prayed that it would be neither as he silently accompanied Janus Crump.

As soon as the pair had left the room Daley's face turned a bright purple. He slammed a fist down on his desk. A glass of whiskey leapt into the air, spilling its contents across the desk. Daley ignored the mess.

'Damn blasted double-crosser,' he snarled, releasing all his pent-up frustration before issuing orders that would effectively get rid of 'Shotgun Murphy' for good. 'Nobody makes a fool out of Highspade Jack Daley and lives to tell the tale.'

After his men had left the room only the mayor and Hymie Weiss remained.

The lawyer was sweating. It was not because of the heat. He nervously mopped his brow. Daley gave his associate a look of disdain.

'Something bothering you, Hymie?' he mocked in a menacing voice.

'This is getting out of hand, Jack,' stuttered the edgy guy. 'I told you that I wanted no part of any more killings. Now you are after getting rid of this guy Juke and letting Brown loose with a heap of dynamite. This whole darned business is going to blow up in our faces.'

Daley emitted a harsh guffaw at the unintended witticism.

'So what do you have in mind, old buddy?' The question was expressed in a friendly tone. It was intended to allay the lawyer's fears, portraying Jack Daley as a fair-minded jasper who was always open to suggestions.

'I'm pulling out on the next stage leaving town.' Weiss turned to leave.

'You can keep any money owed to me. I don't want it.'

'That's mighty generous of you, Hymie.' Daley smirked. 'Bags all packed, then?'

Weiss made for the door. His hand rested on the handle. But he never got to open it. A single shot rang out. The small slug from a concealed pocket gun smashed the lawyer's spine. His back arched, arms lifting as he sank to his knees and keeled over.

'Nobody quits unless I say so,' Daley hissed.

The leering smile on the ruthless official's face was colder than the winter snows. He picked up the fallen glass, then poured himself a generous shot of whiskey and knocked it back. Opening the office door he called down the corridor. 'Pawnee Bill! Up here now. There's some clearing up that requires your expert talents.'

★　★　★

Early the next morning, Laramie rode out of Jacinto with his saddle-bags packed with explosives. He was thankful to have escaped the uneasy atmosphere of the town. There was still a nagging doubt at the back of his mind that Pancho Dominguez might have let something slip.

Spurring his horse to a gentle canter, he was eager to get back to *El Dorado*.

About halfway to Tascosa Canyon the trail passed through a cluster of desiccated trees. Here it was that Digger Brown and his boys had been camped out all night awaiting the arrival of the bogus gunslinger.

In the middle of the clearing stood a dead cottonwood. It was known throughout the district as the Devil's Elbow. Numerous cattle rustlers and horse-thieves had met their ignominious end swinging from the bent arm that stuck out from the main trunk. Bark in the cleft had been rubbed smooth by a legion of swinging felons.

Another noose now hung from the

crossbeam, awaiting the neck of Laramie Juke.

Spread around the clearing hidden from view within the tree cover, Daley's gunmen now waited. Digger Brown stood behind the Devil's Elbow, ready to step out when their quarry arrived. A rifle was clasped against his chest. Not long now.

Five minutes later the steady pounding of hoofs reached his ears.

A raised arm warned his men to be ready. All innocent and oblivious, Laramie entered the clearing from its northern end. At first he did not see the noose swaying in the light morning breeze. Only when Digger Brown stepped into view did he realize that all was not well with the world.

'Rein up there, scumbag!' ordered Brown, pointing his rifle at the startled rider. The call was a signal for his men to emerge from cover. They quickly surrounded the dumbfounded rider, cutting off any retreat. 'Think you could impersonate a famous bounty hunter without being sussed?' sneered Brown.

Before Laramie could respond Janus Crump had removed his holstered pistol while Pieface Bundy extracted the shotgun on the far side of the horse.

'Get him off that nag!' snarled Brown, enjoying the grim moment to the full.

Willing hands dragged Laramie out of the saddle. He was given no chance to escape with Pawnee Bill and a burly tough called Shag Hornbeam gripping each of his arms.

'I guess old Pancho must have blabbed after all,' he muttered with a shake of his head. 'I ought to have known that greaser couldn't keep his big mouth shut.'

'And guess what happens to skunks who try to buck Highspade Jack?' There was no need to wait for a response. Digger's glittering eye flickered towards the ominous hemp necktie. 'No time like the present to give this old Hanging Tree another chance to do its duty.' The affable tone was replaced by a brittle rasp. 'Tie his hands behind his back

then get the bastard mounted.'

Within seconds, Laramie was back astride his horse with the rough collar encircling his neck.

'No need to say your prayers, Judas,' called out Bundy. 'Old Nick has sent out an invitation to a hellfire party with your name on it.' Chuckles all round.

'Then let's send him on his way,' yelled Hornbeam.

A sharp slap on the nag's rump sent the animal bounding away, leaving Juke swinging in the breeze. His legs began to flail in a futile attempt to get free. Laramie had watched a couple of hangings and knew that he had five minutes at the most before his life force would be choked off.

12

Battleground

But all was not lost.

The day before, Saddleback Sutter had ridden out to Tascosa Canyon to inform the Cavendish family that their father was fully recovered and eager to get back to the mine.

'He's been asking the doc to sign him off for the last two days,' said the ostler. 'It's only today that anybody's been coming out this way. I'm taking this roan back to Gil Mossop at Fort Benteen. He's been given a new set of shoes.'

'Is Pa fit enough to travel then?' asked a concerned Shona, offering the guy a cup of coffee and some cake. Sutter accepted them gratefully. 'That was a bad wound and he'd lost a heap of blood.'

'According to the sawbones, old Ben's pulled through remarkably well considering. But he's been causing him no end of bother with his yammering about Jack Daley's underhand practices.' Sutter paused while devouring the tasty offering. 'You folks got a beef with the mayor?'

'He's trying to run us off our claim,' snapped Brad Cavendish angrily. 'That's what got Pa shot up in the first place.'

'It's a long story,' said Shona, not wishing to discuss their situation, even to a steady guy like Saddleback Sutter. 'We'll fill you in when all this has been settled.'

The stableman nodded. It wasn't any of his business, although he could readily sympathize with anybody who rubbed the mayor of Jacinto up the wrong way. 'The doc's worried that it might get back to Daley. Farthing ain't worried for himself. But your pa could find himself in hot water if'n he carries on that way in public.'

'Then we'd best get down there pronto,' urged Brad, 'before he gets

himself locked up.'

After Sutter had left to continue his journey, it was agreed that Randy and Brad should go to collect their father. Thinking he had the law all tied up in his favour meant that Daley would not try anything in public. But just in case, Randy insisted that his sister hold the fort in the canyon.

They set off just as the false dawn was creeping over the eastern fringes of the Dragoon Mountains. Grey shadows offered enough light to pick their way down the narrow ravine. But the two brothers were confident that they could have found their way down the twisting trail blindfold.

As they approached the location of the infamous Devil's Elbow a raucous bellow of macabre glee assailed their ears.

'Sounds like there's a party going on in those trees,' Brad remarked.

Randy's thoughts were more judicious. 'A mite early in the day for a shindig, don't you think?' That hallooing was

categorically not of a friendly nature. Indeed, it sounded decidedly threatening.

He spurred his horse to a canter, pulling up on the edge of the clearing. Dimly shadowed in the greyness of dawn, their presence went unnoticed. But the sight that greeted their ogling peepers was like a picture from hell itself. A ghoulish nightmare come to life.

Half a dozen men with lighted brands were circling the dancing body of what looked like a marionette. But it was a man's body.

The grotesque twist of the Devil's Elbow was silhouetted in the flickering torchlight. The two watchers were stunned by the monstrous scene. It was Brad who was suddenly brought back to the grim reality of the situation in which they now found themselves. His eyes bulged with the brutal shock of recognition.

'That's Laramie swinging on the end of that rope,' he blurted out. Without waiting for any response from his brother,

Brad jammed spurs into his horse's flanks. The animal leapt forward out into the open. Yelling and hollering at the top his voice, the hotheaded young miner palmed his revolver and let fly.

Randy's cry to stop and adopt a more controlled response to the grim set-up was unheard, plucked away by a fitful breeze that rustled across the clearing.

Brad Cavendish, impulsive and reckless, had no thought for the consequences of his madcap dash to save an ally. But hitting a target while firing on the run was wildly speculative. Only if luck was on your side was there any chance of success. He was halfway across the clearing when the executioners realized that they were under attack. And Lady Luck appeared to have stayed home.

None of his shots found their mark.

Brad hunkered down behind his mount's neck as bullets zipped overhead. But with six men returning fire, his was a forlorn hope. Nevertheless, he continued firing until the gun clicked on to an empty chamber.

At that very moment, the horse took a bullet in the neck. It stumbled and went down head over hoofs, throwing its rider off. Brad hit the ground with a heavy thud but was on his feet in moments. He lunged for the rifle on the far side of the dead beast. But it was stuck fast. Desperately, he attempted to haul it free.

Brown and his men now sensed that they had the upper hand.

They spread out, guns blazing until the lone figure pitched forward, his body riddled by at least five bullets. Seeing his brother in such dire straits, Randy Cavendish felt like dashing out himself. But a pragmatic caution forced him to remain cool under pressure. Hunkering down on one knee he proceeded to take careful aim. His first shell struck Janus Crump in the shoulder, spinning him round.

The second removed the top of Pawnee Bill's head. Blood and brains sprayed over those nearest to the dead man.

That was enough to force the gang

back. Panic now threatened to pitch the gang into disarray. One minute they were enjoying a gruesome game of hangman, the next being attacked by hidden forces. A bullet stung Digger Brown's right ear. He let out a squeal of pain. The situation was escalating out of his control.

With two of his men out of action, Brown saw no need to continue the gun battle. He could see one man over on the far side of the clearing, but there might be others close by. The gang had carried out their task. And the life of the Judas was fast being choked out of him.

All the same, Daley was not going to be well pleased with this interference to his plans. The idea had been for the gang to commandeer the dynamite and finish the job that Juke had described. It was a good solid plan that would have effectively settled the matter. That was all up in the air now.

The only thing to do was head back to Jacinto.

Returning fire to keep the intruders

pinned down, Brown shouted for the gang to scramble back to where they had tethered their mounts. Randy let them go. His first concern was to cut down the hanging man. He levered and fired the old Henry three time before the rope parted and Laramie tumbled to the ground.

Randy made a dash for the fallen man, pausing fleetingly to check Brad's still body as he passed. It was clear that Brad was dead. Randy's whole being screamed out in anguish. But this was no time for histrionics. Another man might yet be saved.

A buzzard had settled on the uppermost branches of the hanging tree. Its ominous presence was a portent of ill tidings.

Randy approached the fallen body with trepidation.

Laramie was lying on his stomach. The grisly necklace was stained with blood where it had lacerated the victim's neck.

Gingerly, Randy turned him over. A

choking groan caused him to sigh with relief. Thank the Lord that he had come in time. Quickly but with care he removed the gruesome noose and threw it aside.

'Water, water,' rasped a throaty gurgle. Laramie's pale eyes flickered towards his saviour. 'Seems like . . . this is becoming . . . a habit, old buddy,' he gasped out.

Randy smiled back before returning to the nearest horse to fetch a water bottle which so happened to be that belonging to his deceased brother.

Distraught, Randy stroked Brad's grey features. But he was unable to meet his brother's blank, glassy stare. Grinding his teeth angrily, he swore revenge for this heinous crime with all the passion he could muster.

'I'll make darned certain that the skunks responsible for this pay the full price, little brother. And that's a promise.'

Tears flowed down the stubbly cheeks as he secured the all-important liquid and returned to tend the living.

Once Laramie had been made comfortable, Randy went in search of the victim's horse. It had bolted to the far side of the grove. On the way back he noticed movement over on the edge of the trees. It was the wounded bush-whacker. Crump was endeavouring to seek cover until such time as he could find his own horse.

Randy palmed his revolver as he tentatively approached the wounded man.

'Keep them hands well away from your hogleg,' rapped the miner. 'Any excuse to drill you, mister, would be a pleasure. Now, on your feet!'

Crump had no intention of playing the lionheart. 'It's my shoulder,' he groaned, struggling to rise. His shirt was soaked through with blood. 'You have to help me, or I'll bleed to death.'

'And why should I help a scumbag who helped to kill my brother and string up my buddy?' He snapped the hammer back to full cock.

The ominous click panicked the

gunman. 'I'm just a hired hand brought in by Digger Brown. If'n I'd known things were going to develop into a killing spree like this I'd never have come. Brown told me the job was just collecting rents and bodyguarding for the mayor. Help me out and I'll tell you what Daley plans to set in motion.'

'It better be worth your mangy hide,' scowled Randy whose dander was up and more than ready for terminal retribution. He grabbed the jasper and shook him like a rag doll. 'So come on, spill!'

Crump cowered back. But he could see that his captor was an upright and law-abiding person. So he tried to play the sympathy card.

'Come on, mister,' he whined. 'I can see that you ain't no hard-nosed killer that would shoot a man down in cold blood.' Again he hinted at secrets to be revealed. 'Give me a break and I'll reveal the whole can of worms. Is it a deal?'

Randy hesitated.

Seeing that he had the guy's attention, Crump hurried on with a

tempting opener. 'Your pa has been arrested for the murder of Sheriff Tomlin. He's locked up in the jail right now. They're going to hold a drumhead trial and hang him. It'll be a foregone conclusion. The jury will all be hand-picked by Daley.'

This was a stunning revelation. Randy was dumbfounded.

'You're coming back to *El Dorado* with us,' he informed the anxious bodyguard. 'If'n what you have to say is the truth, then you might come through this with a whole skin. But play me false . . . ' He left the rest unsaid. The implication was obvious.

'I ain't no hero, mister, you got my word,' warbled Crump. 'I'll quit the territory and you won't see me again.' The gunslinger's heavily pock-marked features relaxed. He had won a reprieve.

Some makeshift bandages were torn from the dead killer's shirt and used to temporarily staunch the bleeding in Janus Crump's shoulder. It would

suffice until they returned to the mine. Further examination of the injury showed that the bullet had gone straight through, and it was not life-threatening.

Crump opened up further with some salutary information on the way back to Tascosa Canyon.

It seemed that Brown had intended sending Pawnee Bill with a message for the miners. The half-breed was an excellent tracker. His skill with a bow and arrow had already been displayed to devastating effect.

'He figured the 'breed could get close enough to the cabin to launch an arrow with the message at the door without being spotted by anybody on guard.' Crump was more than ready to expand on Daley's scheme if it would assist in gaining his freedom. 'It would then have been easy for Bill to disappear into the wide blue yonder.' He then went on to outline the contents of the letter.

The gist of the ultimatum was that Ben Cavendish would only be released when the family agreed to surrender all

rights to the mine and its bounteous prize.

After what had since taken place, Randy was in no mood to kowtow to a treacherous snake like Daley. That showed in the grim set of his features. The question thrashing around inside his head during the rest of the journey involved how best to secure his father's freedom without getting him killed in the process. By the time the dejected party reached the cabin, that problem had still to be resolved.

Shona was shocked to witness the carnage that had taken place. Her distress was equal to that of her brother when she saw Brad's body draped over his horse.

'Oh no!' she cried out in despair. 'First Pa and now Brad. Where is all this going to end?'

'With us holding firm to what's rightfully ours,' Randy breathed in a low yet dogged tone. 'That's what we're fighting for. You're still in agreement with that, aren't you, sis?'

'Sure I am,' was Shona's spirited rejoinder as she helped Laramie off his horse.

Randy quickly filled her in on the bloody events of the morning that had left their brother dead.

The only speck of light in the darkness of her despair was that Laramie was still alive. For the second time she became his nurse. His throat and vocal cords had been severely crushed, which meant that only liquids and soft food could be assimilated.

Crump's arm was set in a sling. Then he was securely chained up like a dog in a corner of the room. All the bodyguard could do now was keep quiet and hope that he had done enough to secure his release.

13

Subterfuge

It was three days before Laramie was capable of any speech.

Haltingly, the unfortunate events leading to his near-terminal introduction to the Devil's Elbow came to light. The scar encircling his neck was like a red collar. It was still raw and painful. It would fade in time but was always going to be a potent reminder of how close he had come to death's door.

'So how are we going to handle this?' Randy asked of his buddy when he was at last up and about.

Laramie had been giving the same problem considerable thought as well. His original plan, which had been given to Daley, involved the use of dynamite to destroy the cabin and block up the Tascosa entrance to the mine.

'Why not turn the tables and use the dynamite against the rat?' he suggested.

'Sounds good to me,' answered a rejuvenated Randy Cavendish.

'And don't be forgetting me,' Shona butted in, anxious not to be left out. 'I'm in on this caper too.' Laramie tried to raise an objection but the girl cut off his protestations before a single word could be uttered. 'With poor Brad buried outside now, you guys will be needing all the help you can get to free Pa.'

There was no denying that every extra gun would be a bonus. Laramie concurred, if a touch reluctantly. Then he explained what he had in mind.

'I have three sticks.' He tapped the saddle-bag containing the deadly contents. 'That ought to be enough to cause a noisy diversion enabling you both to break Ben out of jail.'

Janus Crump had been listening intently to the plans being discussed. *Hear all, see all and say nothing!* A valuable adage that had served him well in the past.

Laramie had noticed the sly look

creasing the varmint's ugly kisser, but he didn't say anything to the others as he continued to explain what he had in mind.

'Daley will expect us to come in from the south to bust your pa out of the pokey. So he'll concentrate all his men on watching that end of Jacinto. But we come in on the north side, where there will be no opposition to stop us. By the time the skunk has sussed out what's happened, we will be long gone.'

Shona was enthused by the idea.

Randy was equally smitten. 'We'll thrash out the details over supper, and set out first thing in the morning.' He threw a look of concern at his buddy. 'You recovered enough to handle this, Laramie?'

The cowboy gingerly fingered the tender scarring on his neck. He winced at the touch. 'Maybe I could use a couple more days to get my strength back.' He considered for a moment. 'It's Friday now. Reckon I'll be all set to go on Monday if'n that's OK with you guys.'

'The extra time will give us the opportunity to iron out any snags,' mused Randy, pouring them both a shot of moonshine. 'Here's to freeing Pa and running that skunk out of Jacinto on a rail.' Glasses were raised and toasts saluted.

Over in the corner, Janus Crump was becoming restive. He wanted to raise the subject of his release but was hesitant in case the submission was rejected. It was the bogus Shotgun Murphy who came to his assistance.

'I reckon this critter has learned his lesson,' observed Laramie. 'No sense in giving him free board and lodging. You guys all right for him to skedaddle now that he's let us know Daley's plans?'

Without waiting for the others to OK the proposal, Crump jumped in to assure them of his intention to quit the territory.

'Got me the chance of some good honest work on a ranch in the San Antonio country. Once I leave here, you won't see me for dust.'

'Be assured, Crump,' Randy threatened, wagging his six-shooter in the jigger's face, 'if'n we do catch sight of your worthless hide, it'll be a one-way ticket to hell from Mr Remington here.'

Shona moved across and untied the prisoner. Crump lurched to his feet, rubbing the stiffness from his limbs.

'Your horse is outside,' snapped Randy. 'Now git!'

Crump did not need a second telling. He was through the door in the blink of an eye. The pounding of hoofs informed the occupants of the cabin that the jasper had no intentions of lingering in Tascosa Canyon.

'Think he'll head for Texas?' enquired Shona.

Laramie shook his head. 'Never in a million years. Guys like that never change. Come tomorrow morning, he'll be spilling our plans to Daley and hoping for a cut of the action.'

Randy was dumbfounded. 'So why in thunder did you suggest we let him go?'

Laramie replied with a sneaky smirk,

and then revealed that he had been hatching a crafty plan.

'Daley will think we're hitting the town on Monday and coming in from the north, true?' He was rewarded with a couple of sceptical nods. 'What if'n we were to pull this stunt on Sunday, and come in from the east through the jumble of corrals and stables to give us extra cover? And we'll arrive early when they're all sleeping off the excesses of Saturday night.'

The cloud of puzzlement instantly lifted as all became clear as a mountain stream. Randy slapped his buddy on the back. 'That's a brilliant ruse. Now why didn't I think of it?'

'Does that really need an answer?' mocked Shona with a sisterly nudge in the ribs.

They all burst out laughing. Suddenly, the future looked much more attractive. There were some tough times ahead. Releasing Ben Cavendish was not going to be easy. But they felt equal to the challenge.

Sunday morning couldn't come soon enough.

The next day was spent going over the plan of action. Laramie insisted that each of them, including himself, should recite exactly what their role entailed. In essence it required meticulous timing to ensure that the custodians holding the prisoner had vacated the jailhouse.

Explosions behind the council offices would provide the essential distraction. Loud and alarming, but not injurious, like a dog whose bark is worse than its bite. Nothing would be gained by destroying property that would be required once the present incumbent had been ousted.

Randy and his sister had been assigned to take care of the jail break.

Laramie would create the distraction with the dynamite. But he also had his own agenda, which concerned a showdown with Highspade Jack Daley, although this had not been made public. The most important element of the plan was for the Cavendish clan to get away safely

and return to Tascosa Canyon. Once Laramie was sure that this had been successfully accomplished he could bring his own scheme to fruition.

Time passed slowly as the hands of the clock crept round. All three participants in this dangerous enterprise were jumpy and on edge. Weapons were cleaned and checked, then cleaned again. Numerous cigarettes were smoked and cups of coffee drunk. But no alcohol!

Laramie insisted that they needed to stay alert. 'Time enough to open a fresh batch of your moonshine once Daley's scheme has been squashed,' he assured them.

14

Coming to Blows

The tiny army of three halted on a low knoll outside Jacinto. The trip from Tascosa Canyon had been timed for them to arrive just as dawn was breaking. Long shadows still cloaked the terrain in a thick embrace. But there was now sufficient light to carry out their perilous task.

No other human presence stirred in the town.

Laramie smiled. A look of grim tenacity tightened the muscles of his face. This was just as he had hoped it would be. He now had to hope and pray that Janus Crump had taken the bait hook, line and sinker.

A lone dog out for an early morning prowl slunk across their path. It was the only presence to disturb the tranquillity.

However, all that was about to change.

'I'll come in from that side.' Laramie pointed to a cluster of shacks and vacant lots over to his right. Even though they were well beyond hearing range, Laramie's delivery was barely above a whisper.

'Remember! When you're in position behind the jailhouse, don't make your move until the guards leave. We don't know how many of Daley's gang have been deputized. I figure there'll be at least two in there. They won't be expecting us. But that will alter rapidly once they have recovered from the shock.'

Somewhat impatiently, Randy signalled his understanding. Now that the moment of truth had arrived, the tension was palpable. The plan had been reviewed numerous times already. All that the big miner wanted now was to get on with it and secure his pa's freedom.

Laramie squeezed Shona's arm as she made to follow her brother. An

unspoken determination to succeed passed between them. The next time they met, their hope was that they would be ready to challenge Jack Daley's hold over them.

As the two Cavendish siblings faded into the murky gloom, their aim was to circle round and come in from the west. Laramie nudged his own mount down the shallow grade, keeping a sharp lookout for any suspicious movement. Entering the squalid collection of hutments, he was looking for some that had been abandoned. The last thing he wanted was to purposely place any innocent occupier in peril.

An old derelict barn offered the ideal spot from which to launch his assault. Once inside, he set about priming the three sticks of dynamite. Lady Luck had further displayed her favours by providing a number of empty water barrels.

After filling three of them with damped-down straw, the sticks were given fuses of varying lengths. The idea was for them to explode in sequence allowing

Laramie to get back under cover before the first one blew. Regular explosions at set intervals would create the most chaos among the occupants of the building.

Having cut the fuse wire to the correct lengths and affixed them to the sticks, he then ventured out into the open with the first barrel.

In the nick of time he managed to drop down behind it when the swaying form of an early riser appeared out of the gloom. Luckily, the guy's head was sunk on to his chest. He was clearly suffering from a hangover. Laramie allowed the guy to pass before emerging once more.

Speed was now of the essence as more people might well appear before too long. Upending the barrel, he rolled it over to one corner of the council offices. He struck a vesta and applied the flame to the longest fuse. The other two barrels were quickly rolled into place at strategic points along the back wall.

As he turned away, making a hasty

retreat back to the barn, disaster struck.

Too intent on looking around to ensure he was still alone, Laramie barged straight into a hulking figure. Both men went down in a heap of tangled limbs.

'Ugh! You clumsy bastard!' cussed the surprised individual, gasping for breath. 'Why in thunder don't you watch where you're going, mister?'

Laramie was the first on his feet. Even in the dim light of early morning he recognized the rotund figure of Pieface Bundy. The heavy-set tough was not the fleetest of movers, but he recovered quickly.

'You!' he snapped as recognition dawned. 'Crump said you weren't coming until tomorrow.'

Laramie gritted his teeth. So his theory about the two-faced villain had been right all along. But this was no time for such ruminations. Already Bundy was reaching for his revolver. Gunplay at this early stage in the proceedings would ruin everything. Fortunately, the lard-bucket's excess girth and spinning head slowed his actions.

Putting him out of action was now a vital necessity. Without thought Laramie drew a thin stiletto fastened to his left boot. He had regularly practised throwing the deadly blade, but had never had cause to use it. Until now.

In a single lithe shift, he flicked the knife underhand at the corpulent figure. He could hardly miss such a gigantic target. It was a perfect throw. Bundy gurgled as the long thin shaft penetrated his chest. A scrabbling hand gripped the handle as blood poured from his gaping mouth.

Life quickly ebbed from the fatally injured man as the last gasps of air hissed out of a punctured lung. Then he lost the battle. His assailant removed the knife and slipped it back into the boot sheath. This was not the time to reflect on his killing of the bodyguard. Nor was there time to conceal the corpse.

Already the seconds were slipping away fast. The first stick would blow in a few minutes. But at least Daley was now one man down.

Laramie hurried back to the barn to await the expected panic-stricken evacuation of the offices when the dynamite blew. He could only pray and hope that Daley had spent the night carousing there along with his cronies. According to information he had gleaned during his short sojourn in Jacinto, that was normal Saturday night practice for the mayor.

Any entertainment of the female variety was ordered beforehand from the Red Garter Men's Club run by Cattle Annie. The house madame was suspected of accepting rustled steers in exchange for her erotic favours.

Time hung heavy as Laramie waited anxiously. His nerves were on edge as he willed the first stick of dynamite to do its work.

Then a single muted blast shook the rotting timbers of the old barn. Dust filtered down on to the watcher's head. Laramie was gripping his revolver so tightly that the knuckles of his hand blanched white. His eyes glowered at

the rear door of the council chamber as he waited for the action to commence. The air was filled with slivers of charred wood and smoking flecks of straw.

Moments later the other sticks exploded in rapid succession, adding to the noisy confusion. As intended, no damage had been occasioned to the building. The diversionary tactics appeared to have worked perfectly. Now it was time for the second part of the plan to be instigated.

On the far side of the main street, Randy and his sister were also on tenterhooks in the narrow alley abutting the jailhouse. The only problem they had encountered was a barking mutt, which had been effectively driven off with a couple of well-placed stones. Now they were also apprehensively waiting for the action to commence.

The first explosion came as something of a shock, the eerie silence being abruptly shattered by a loud report and a flash that speared the gloom. Fleeting shadows could be seen through the

grime of the jailhouse window. The custodians threw open the door and emerged on to the street. Ashen faces registered total incredulity.

'Holy cow!' The startled expletive spat from the mouth of Digger Brown. 'What in thunderation was that?' Quizzical looks passed between the two men. The second man immediately realized that he had been duped. He gulped in trepidation.

Randy immediately recognized Janus Crump. His eyes narrowed. A twisted look of hatred clouded his salient features. His palmed gun was aimed at the double-crossing skunk's back.

It was Shona who prevented an impulsive act that would have stymied their ultimate objective. She laid a restraining hand on Randy's gun hand.

'Leave that for when it's needed,' she hissed in his ear. 'Our job is to rescue Pa, not start our own conflict.'

Her brother's face relaxed. He knew she was right.

'I saw red for a moment there,' he apologized. 'It won't happen again.'

'It's them damned prospectors!' shouted Brown running across the street. 'They're attacking the mayor's office.' Crump followed, displaying rather less enthusiasm. This was not supposed to happen for another twenty-four hours.

Once they had disappeared round the corner Randy moved to the front of the jail, the door of which had been left ajar in the panic. Gingerly he stepped inside the spartan office, gun held at the ready. It was empty. A large iron stove dominated the room. On its hob sat a bubbling coffee pot, but Randy's main concern was the door at the rear leading into the cell block. He hurried across. A twist of the handle revealed it to be locked. A curse issued from between his pursed lips. Now he would have to blast it open.

'You keep watch while I break this darned thing open,' he said to Shona. 'Let's hope those jiggers don't hear this.'

Stepping back a pace, he aimed his gun at the heavy lock. The discharge was ear-shattering in the closed space.

Wafting the smoke away, the shooter could see that the pistol shot had made barely any impression. A second shot fared no better.

He growled out a lurid imprecation.

'What the heck are we going to do now?' came the angry cry. Being far more patient and composed than her brother, Shona had sussed out the answer in an instant.

'Use that shotgun,' she said, pointing to a rack of long guns on the wall.

Hefting a sawn-off Greener, Randy stepped well back and let fly with both barrels. The lock exploded into a myriad of fragments.

Discarding the weapon, Randy burst through into the inner sanctum where his father was anxiously gripping the bars. Two more shots from his pistol effectively broke the less resilient lock of the cell door.

'Thank the Lord you've come,' enthused Ben Cavendish, pushing out into the corridor. 'Those critters were all set to hang me on a trumped-up

charge of murdering Sheriff Tomlin.'

'No time for discussions now, Pa.' Randy ushered the older man back into the main office. 'We have some horses round the side of the jail. An old buddy of mine is keeping the rest of these varmints busy while we make good our escape.'

'Who is he?' asked his curious father as they emerged from the jail.

'A guy that I helped out in Dodge City last year,' replied Randy, urging his father into the alley. 'Now he's returning the favour.'

Digger Brown and Crump were about to enter the alley leading round to the rear of the council offices when they heard the gunfire to their rear. The sheriff skidded to a halt. He suddenly realized that the explosions were a ploy to draw the guards away and so enable a breakout to be achieved. Swinging on his heel, the tin star witnessed the prisoner and his two rescuers outside the jail.

His response was a couple of quick

shots. They went wide but were enough to force the trio down behind a horse trough, where they were effectively trapped.

As only Shona and Randy were armed, their father could only keep his head down as bullets began to pepper their meagre shelter.

Brother and sister responded by dispatching their own lead-filled messages to the aggressors. Brown and his men took cover on the far side behind some cotton bales. But they now held the whip hand. Other members of Daley's odious pack of brigands now appeared down the steps of the council offices at the far end. Led by Shag Hornbeam they advanced cautiously along the sidewalk.

All the prospectors could do was pray for a miracle. That was the only thing that would save them now.

15

Snake Eyes

And that is exactly what happened.

Suddenly, gunfire erupted from down the street. It was not directed at the trapped fugitives. Saddleback Sutter and his assistant Henry Crabbe were steadily making their way along the far side of the street. By taking advantage of the cover offered, they were able to pump regular shots at Daley's men, keeping them pinned down.

Hornbeam tried to make a run for it but was cut down before he reached his horse. The others backed off, recognizing that discretion was the better part of valour.

More of the town's citizens had decided to rise up against the tyrannical rule of Highspade Jack Daley and his minions. The plucky retaliation being

brought about by the Cavendish clan had clearly spurred the rest of the town into action.

Just at the right moment.

A shot came from an upstairs window of the dressmaker's, where Maisie Dobson had been observing the dire situation with impotent fury. The sudden intervention of Sutter had spurred her into action. This was the first time the young woman had ever fired a gun in anger. Her shots went well wide of their targets. But they augmented the sudden yet welcome insurgence.

Shona cheered. A hand lifted to acknowledge her friend's involvement.

Seeing that the tables were being turned on them, a couple of Daley's men, including Janus Crump, ran for their horses. Spurring off down towards the north end of Jacinto, they were hoping to make a clean getaway. But their escape was thwarted by others who had found the courage to stand up and oppose Jack Daley's repressive administration.

This fresh group of irate citizens was

led by Doc Farthing.

The men quickly pushed out a couple of wagons, effectively blocking off that end of the street. Sheltering behind the makeshift barricade, the newly enthused citizens poured a ferocious hail of lead at their much hated but recently feared overlords.

The escapers didn't stand a chance. Three bodies bit the dust, each perforated by a half-dozen bullets. The others panicked. They swung their mounts away and huddled behind any cover available, eager to avoid the sudden threat to their easy lifestyle.

Only Kid Mancos and Brown were left. The Aussie hardcase hurled a scathing imprecation at his cowardly sidekicks before backing down the alley adjoining the council offices.

'I'm getting out of here,' shouted the frightened Kid above the cacophony of blasting firearms. 'Things in this town are getting too hot to handle.'

He had only managed to insert one boot in the stirrup of his tethered but

jumpy horse before a menacing voice cut through the overpowering din.

'Hold it right there.' The stentorian command stayed the nervy Kid in his tracks. 'Where's Daley skulking?' The brittle demand was punched out with venom.

Laramie stepped out into the open. His gun was holstered but the bearing of the determined cowboy was anything but casual. His hand hovered above the butt of his Colt Peacemaker, acquired gratis during his brief period while impersonating Shotgun Murphy.

'Last I seen of him was in the office upstairs.' Mancos was now thoroughly cowed and eager to comply. His hands were raised in surrender. 'He must be still up there.'

Brown was made of sterner stuff. He growled out a baleful curse at the snivelling brat. Then he went for his gun.

Laramie had anticipated the move. His own hand dropped. Both guns rose together. But Brown was in too much of a rush. Laramie had learned the

deadly art of triggernometry from the hand and mouth of none other than Wild Bill Hickok. The legendary law officer of Abilene had told him that a brief moment taken to aim would always beat a hurried draw. All it took was nerve and a steady hand.

The bodyguard's bullet went wide, smashing one of the few remaining windows in the old barn.

Laramie's gun spat flame and death before Brown was given a second chance. The Australian tough was dead before his body hit the dirt.

Kid Mancos could only stare open-mouthed. His hands grabbed for the new sun that was now pitching over the scalloped moulding of the Dragoon Mountains.

'D-don't shoot, mister,' he burbled, almost in tears.

Laramie held the lily-livered bandit with a menacing glower. 'You have one minute to leave town,' he growled. 'And if'n I see your fleabitten carcass around here again, it'll get the same treatment

as I dished out to this one-eyed skunk.'

Mancos did not need a second bidding. He leapt into the saddle. Spurs dug deep, the sorrel reared up on its hind legs before making a spirited dash for open country.

'Now for you, Mister Highspade,' Laramie spat out in a lurid snarl of hate.

Cautiously, he headed for the back stairs of the council office. Smoke drifted from the shattered barrels, wisps of burning straw were still floating in the air. Laramie cut through the opaque screen and quickly mounted the stairway, levering out the spent cartridges from his revolver before reloading.

A wary nudge and the upper door swung open. His sharp ears picked up the rustle of papers down the corridor. A forbidding smile passed over his dour features. It had to be Daley, gathering his goods together before making a play for freedom.

Back on the main street, those desperadoes who were still drawing

breath had already given up the fight. Doc Farthing and Saddleback Sutter had relieved them of their hardware and had herded them over to the jail.

Maisie Dobson emerged from her establishment feeling rather shaken but undaunted. She hurried over to her friend. The two women clung to one another, tears of relief flooding down their cheeks.

'Haven't I earned some of that?' enquired a relieved Randy Cavendish in a mildly whimsical tone of voice. Maisie coloured as her paramour joined them.

Shona discreetly sidled away to join her father who was dusting himself down, eager to join the fray. 'About time that young fella settled down,' he remarked with a knowing look at his daughter as if to say, *what about you, gal?*

Shona gave the remark an imperious sniff as they left the couple to flap and coo like a pair of turtle doves.

'Seems like I'm too late to join in the action,' complained Ben as Doc Farthing and the other men arrived with their

subdued captives.

But Shona was not listening. The worried girl was more concerned with the whereabouts of Laramie Juke. Gunfire from behind the council offices gave a stark reminder that the battle for Jacinto was not yet over.

Laramie cat-footed down the corridor to the end room where Daley had conducted all his nefarious deals. Peeping round the open door, he was accorded a full view of the duplicitous varmint bending over his safe. He was removing the contents. Packets of banknotes were being stuffed into a bag.

It was clear that the mayor was in a hurry to leave. His back was to the new arrival, who stole into the room as silent as a church mouse. Then Laramie slammed the door shut. Daley almost fell over with the shock. He spun round.

A revolver was pointing in his direction.

'You figuring on taking a vacation, Jack?' The genial pleasantry concealed an edge of steel. 'The boys ain't gonna

be too pleased about you running out on them.' Then another thought occurred to the wily cowpoke as he peered out of the front window. 'Although it would appear that the ones still left have other things on their mind.'

Daley knew that the game was up. But he still tried to dig his way out of the hole in which he was now trapped.

'We can do a deal, Shotgun . . . or whatever your name is,' wheedled the craven tinhorn. 'There's enough dough here for us both to live the high life. More than a lowly cowboy could earn in a lifetime. So what do you say?' He lifted out a wad of greenbacks, waving them in a futile effort to escape justice.

Laramie shook his head in mocking reproof. 'You ain't trying to bribe me, are you, *Mister* Mayor? Not exactly the honourable actions of a candidate for high office.'

'Cut out the smooth talk, mister,' Daley snapped, in an excess of desperate bravado. 'Are you up for this?'

Laramie considered the question for

a moment before playing his hand.

'Tell you what we're going to do,' he said, adopting an even-toned reply. 'You won't remember me, Jack. But last year in Dodge you cheated me out of all the dough that I'd earned on a trail drive.' The one-time braggart attempted a blustering denial, but Laramie held up a hand, effectively silencing him. 'Poker wasn't my game, as I discovered to my cost, but craps is. So that's what we'll play. Just one throw each, winner takes all.'

He dug out a set of dice and flicked the numbered cubes into the air, then caught them in a deft manoeuvre.

'What's the bet?' asked the puzzled gambler.

'I have here an affidavit for you to sign that all future rights to the diggings in Tascosa Canyon are hereby transferred to the Cavendish family. We know that you tried to pull a stunt regarding the occupation clause. That condition would lapse once you had indeed occupied the land for a full year.

Time enough for the family to extract a substantial amount from the mine. But the work might take a sight longer than they figured. This document gives them a firm guarantee — in perpetuity, as the lawyers say.'

'And what do I get out of this if'n I win?'

'You can leave here by the back door, taking your ill-gotten gains with you. And you will have firm control of the mine.' Laramie's tone now became brittle. 'That's my deal. And I don't reckon you have much choice but to accept it.'

The two adversaries eyed one another.

'OK, let's play,' hissed Daley, grabbing the dice. A venomous smirk gave his normally handsome visage an ugly twist. 'So what are the odds?'

'Seven or eleven wins. But Snake Eyes beats all.'

The cardsharp responded with a curt nod of the head.

Holding the other man's gaze, High-spade tapped the lucky ace stuck in his

hatband. Manipulating the dice, he blew into his closed fist before launching them across the floor. Bouncing and joggling like a couple of mischievous puppies, the dice hit the wall as required by the rules of the game, then jumped back. Both players followed their progress with mesmerized attention.

Five followed by a six made a score of eleven.

Daley slammed a bunched fist into the palm of his hand in glee. 'Yes!' he exclaimed with animated fervour.

'Good throw,' Laramie congratulated his opponent. 'But is it good enough?'

Now it was his turn. The chances of throwing a Snake Eyes — double one, were odds that no gambler would have accepted.

Once again the dice flew. Time stood still as they cavorted and danced, jostling for position. And then . . . the unrealistic occurred.

Snake Eyes it was!

Daley's eyes bulged in disbelief. He swallowed hard. Then he remembered

the bet. He could still ride away with a substantial grubstake. Laramie pushed the affidavit across the desk for him to sign. In a trance, Jack Daley affixed his name. Then he picked up the heavy bag and made to leave.

'Not so fast,' rapped the winner of the bet. 'Where are you going?'

'We had a deal, remember?'

Laramie scratched his head in bafflement. 'Can't say that I do. You have a lot to answer for, tinhorn. When a proper court of law learns about all your evil collusions, I reckon you'll be lucky to get a job as a saloon swamper. That is if'n the judge don't send you down.'

'Why you double-crossing . . . '

Daley's left hand reached across, grabbing for the tiny Dexter Smith single-shot .22 in his vest pocket. The small gun had done for Hymie Weiss. It would now eradicate this troublemaker. But Laramie was awaiting such a ploy. His own revolver answered with devastating effect. Daley clutched at his stomach. A look of pained surprise creased his face.

'How did you manage it . . . ?' His breathing was ragged and short. 'The Snake Eyes?'

The craps player responded with a cunning smile. Deftly he flung the dice at the wall again. The result: Snake Eyes.

'Loaded dice!'

'Made to my own personal specifications,' agreed the pitcher.

As Daley was struggling to draw in his final breath, there sounded a hurried dash along the corridor.

Not knowing if it was friend or foe, Laramie hurriedly scrambled behind the door. It flew open. The newcomer stood there, a scream of terror erupting from her mouth. Shona grabbed for the doorjamb to prevent herself from falling. Then Laramie emerged from his place of concealment.

The two fell into each other's arms.

'I thought he had got you,' the girl gasped out, fresh tears trickling down her smooth cheeks.

'Take more than a chiselling tinhorn

241

to finish off Laramie Juke,' he averred holding her close.

'Is this nightmare really over?' she said in a voice cracking with pent-up emotion.

'Sure hope so, honey,' he replied as they quickly made to vacate the killing ground.

Down on the main street people were milling about, unable to comprehend that the tyranny of the last six months was over at last.

As an ex-member of the town council, prior to being voted off by Daley's paid lackeys, Doc Farthing was trying to bring some organisation to the chaos. Ben Cavendish had offered his help.

The two lovers had just emerged from the council offices on the far side of the plaza. They were joined by Maisie Dobson and her consort.

'How do you two fancy a double wedding this fall?' Randy suggested, giving Maisie's trim waist a squeeze.

Laramie considered the proposal for a moment before answering.

'That will be fine by me,' he said with a cheeky smile. 'Just so long as it's not going to be a shotgun wedding.'

THE END

We do hope that you have enjoyed reading this large print book.

Did you know that all of our titles are available for purchase?

We publish a wide range of high quality large print books including:
Romances, Mysteries, Classics
General Fiction
Non Fiction and Westerns

Special interest titles available in large print are:
The Little Oxford Dictionary
Music Book, Song Book
Hymn Book, Service Book

Also available from us courtesy of Oxford University Press:
Young Readers' Dictionary
(large print edition)
Young Readers' Thesaurus
(large print edition)

For further information or a free brochure, please contact us at:
Ulverscroft Large Print Books Ltd.,
The Green, Bradgate Road, Anstey,
Leicester, LE7 7FU, England.
Tel: (00 44) **0116 236 4325**
Fax: (00 44) **0116 234 0205**

TRACE TAKES A HAND

Owen G. Irons

Years ago, the Arista gang stole fifty thousand dollars — only for one member to escape with the whole haul . . . The traitor, Luke Cason, is living quietly with his daughter Sally — until he is abducted by his former associates, seeking both vengeance and the money. Meanwhile, Texas state marshal Trace Cavanagh is staking plenty on a big gamble: taking two convicts from the penitentiary to assist him in hunting the gang. When their path crosses with Sally's, lawkeepers and lawbreakers alike must join forces to track down the deadly Aristas . . .

BITTER TRAIL

Dale Graham

Lazy Jake Fontell and his partner Buffalo Bob have gone into the freighting business. Approaching El Paso, they have no idea of the troubles they will encounter after coming to the aid of a dying Mexican. Before succumbing to his injuries, the grandee gives the pair a map detailing the location of an icon that was worn by the legendary Aztec leader Montezuma. A secret revolutionary group has sworn to overthrow the Mexican government — and he who wields the headdress wields the power . . .

REVEREND COLT

James Clay

When his wife Christina was murdered by a man she had tried to help, Preacher Paul Colten's idealism died in the dust — and he took the first steps on the road to becoming the gunfighter known as Reverend Colt . . . Arriving in Grayson, Colten finds a town under the brutal control of a wealthy rancher. Though he admires the local newspaper's stand against corruption, he knows that Grayson's rulers will not be stopped by editorials. Reverend Colt's skills with a weapon will be put to the ultimate test.

THE IRON HORSE

Dale Graham

Josiah Wakefield and Dan Sturgis are young Civil War veterans employed by the Union Pacific Railroad. Their job: to hunt down the hired gunmen who are wrecking the UPR's supply trains. It's suspected that someone is trying to slow the railroad's westward progress . . . After a vicious firefight on the Nebraska plains, the pair's continued pursuit takes them to the dissolute city of Omaha — where, between their new acquaintance Bill Hickok, and the deadly city marshal Deke Pritchett, their troubles are only just beginning . . .

THE OKLAHOMBRES

Steve Hayes and Ben Bridges

Bill Doolin is a loving husband and devoted father, who had never killed another man. But he becomes a target for every U.S. Marshal in Oklahoma Territory when the people hail him as 'King of the Outlaws'. When Doolin and his gang, the Oklahombres, raise hell throughout the Twin Territories of Oklahoma and the Indian Nations, Marshal E.D. Nix sends three hundred of his best men out with orders to finish them. However, the Oklahombres are determined to be living legends — or die trying . . .

LATE FOR GETTYSBURG

Vance Tillman

Though the Civil War is over, former Confederate soldier Eugene Wyeth refuses to forgive and forget. Living under an assumed name with a price on his head, he wanders the country, anticipating a bounty hunter around every corner. But when his old comrade-in-arms Rattlesnake Jack is shot, Wyeth must risk exposure and ride into town to seek help. With the powerful Kirby Taylor and his gang of gunslingers determined to stand in Wyeth's way, there is trouble looming.